CW00688028

KILL ME NOW

Christopher Ridley

Oh calm down, it's just LA.

for my family

INTRO

To our wonderful readers:

Thank you for joining us on this amazing adventure. What began as a simple curiosity into a confounding event evolved into what lies in the pages before you. We sought out each of the players with the intent of giving them space to present their views in their voice, and in return received these surprising and oftentimes meandering musings. Since our goal was to allow each individual to express themselves however they felt best, we have not edited their submissions so some content may seem unsavory to certain people. But to quote the American icon Nicole Kidman, and her criminally underappreciated role in *To Die For*, "It's nice to live in a country where life, liberty, and all the rest still stand for something."

And for our more thoughtful readers who might query "But friendly editors, how could some of them actually write their own stories?", our answer is three simple words: Suspension of disbelief.

With that, we hope you find these as probing and insightful as we have. Regardless (because despite what Merriam-Webster says, "irregardless" is not a word but a joke made by Tina Fey to laugh at a character who didn't realize that it's not a real word), please enjoy responsibly.

Fondly,

The Editors

THE MURDER

I remember when I was younger how scandalous it felt to walk down the middle of the road during a neighborhood block party. On any other day my mother would've been screaming from the front porch "GET OUT OF THE STREET!", her pitch so high it seemed her words would injure me more than any passing car. But on those summer nights when orange cones lined both entrances to Bradford Drive I marched straight down that dividing line like a balance beam, traffic safety be damned.

Now, some twenty or so years later, I find myself laying on a winding mountain road in front of my somewhat new Los Angeles home and it is far less thrilling. The cement is cold and lined with a dewy film, the result of the chilly January night air mixing with the daytime sun. As I stare up at my house it looks strangely unfamiliar. The basics of course are all the same—the off-white color and the navy trim around the two sliding glass doors that serve as the eyes of the house. The boxy exterior hiding the weird, split-level interior designed with three floors separated by only a handful of steps each. But obnoxious details that I swear I'd never seen before taunt me. How can there be no rain gutters on the front of the house? Are those two flimsy joists really the only support for the balcony off the sliding glass doors? And why WHY would anyone have an indoor vaulted ceiling with a flat top roof?

My therapist would point out that my fixation with the design flaws of my house despite my current situation is another example of my evasiveness. By laboring over the minutiae I can avoid confronting the primary issue that resulted in my body being sprawled on the pavement in the middle

1

of the night. I would argue that these seemingly petty inconveniences could someday grow into primary issues themselves and thus deserve an equal amount of attention, to which she would contend that my rationalization comes across as defensive. We would then stare at each other in silence for the remaining ten minutes of my session until I traipsed out in a childish victory.

But as much as it pains me to admit that she's right—I hate her—I cannot ignore any longer that this situation is dire. My limbs are entirely unresponsive. What I thought was a layer of mid-winter dew is, I'm now realizing, a puddle of my own blood seeping between the fingers of my left hand. The shadowy figure looking down from my balcony has disappeared. Stanley Kowalski, my indoor cat, has stepped through the broken glass of the sliding door and is walking along the railing, and I can tell he's seriously considering jumping. I'm bloated and only wearing my old green American Apparel briefs, the ones with the stretched-out waistband. Bleak.

What's even more maddening is that I shouldn't be here. Not just because, like everyone else, I think I'm a good person. Which I do. And I am. But more because I know better than to let myself end up this way. I watch a lot of movies, many of them the scary slasher type where people are stalked and chased through dimly lit buildings. I have borne witness to a multitude of sneak attacks and figured out the best recourse for a variety of circumstances. I've planned escape routes in every residence I've settled into, from dorm rooms to apartments to this very home. I keep a baseball bat in the closet and the butcher's block of knives on the counter closest to the kitchen's entrance. And yet here I lay.

To recap the evening, I had gone to bed early because the penne alla vodka that Postmates delivered from La Scala was sitting heavy in my stomach (full disclosure: I felt incredibly bloated and was regretting my eat-my-feelings dinner choice). I curled under the covers with Stanley Kowalski already nestled at the foot of the bed—just far enough away that we weren't touching, but close enough that I had to contort myself if I wanted to shift positions. His snoring echoed through the silent house. It's quite impressive how loud a noise can emerge from such a tiny animal. Rather than the ador-able purring sound movies tell us exude from cats, his was more like an eighty-year-old chain-smoker wheezing as their nurse refills the oxygen tank. But no need to feel sorry for him; Stanley Kowalski doesn't have any health issues. It's just his dramatic personality craving attention. I can't im-agine where he learned that.

I convinced myself his labored breathing was the equivalent of a sound machine and was just about to coo myself to sleep when what sounded like a floorboard creaking under the weight of a person crept in from the living room. It wasn't loud enough to startle me, and yet I still felt compelled to investigate—the first of many wise decisions. Rising out of bed with a sleep-ing cat at your feet, especially this particular cat, is no easy task though. If you simply throw your legs over the side like a caveman, you'll endure a venomous stare, probable hissing and possibly a muted attack full of scratching and even a tiny nip. So with the stealth of Catherine Zeta-Jones in *Entrapment*, I maneuvered my way out of bed without disturbing Stanley Kowalski: my left leg rotated out at the hip until it became parallel with the headboard, then I pivoted at the waist to my right so as to keep the other leg immobile; then I slithered headfirst off the bed, using my hands to brace the floor as I rolled from my shoulders onto my back. The grand finale was my right leg gliding out from under the duvet undetected. I rose in a silent flourish, then snuck out into the hallway. Please note that I did not stop at the closet to retrieve the baseball bat kept handy for protection, the second of my wise decisions for those of you keeping track. I did however throw on my cherry-blossom-covered silk kimono robe.

I tip-toed from my bedroom into the dining area, almost naked and not yet afraid. I kept the robe open so it billowed behind me as I walked. It makes me feel very chic and important. Last summer I was inspired by *The Witches of Eastwick* and *The Birdcage*, so invested in a lot of flowing robes and vacation pants. As I wafted through, I glanced into the kitchen to make sure the door to the patio was closed (it was), and continued on my way. The expensive and very dangerous Wolfgang Puck knives waited diligently for me to unsheathe any one of them, but my third mistake sat with them as I continued on my ignorant way completely unarmed.

I took a brief pause at my gorgeous wood dining table I got at one of HD Buttercup's amazing warehouse sales—I hate to gloat, but I got it for under a thousand dollars, and I swear it's full solid wood and seats eight people. It's so beautiful; if I wasn't dying in the street, I'd invite you over just to show it off. It's my favorite thing I own, other than Stanley Kowalski of course.

Back to the sad gay version of *Dead Man Walking*. I paused at the table to reminisce about the night before. It wasn't my proudest moment. I really thought I'd moved on, but there I was, spiraling down the familiar path of paranoid insecurity. I've been lonely, I'll admit it, and wanted someone to comfort me, make me feel good about myself again. The mistakes I've made in many of my relationships swirled around in my head, taunting me into self-destructive thoughts, but instead of trying to make amends, I brought over the one person who's a constant reminder of how much of a shithead I am. The worst part is, I wasn't even most upset by what we did. The real heartache was that we defiled my wonderful table.

The previous night's events stung long enough so I shook them off and continued on my sojourn to investigate the strange noise. There was no sign of any disturbance as I looked down into the living room, the sliding glass doors opening the opposite wall to the night outside. I was taken for a moment and once again distracted by the stillness of my neighborhood. Fog rolled under the streetlight and normally I would find it eerie akin to an establishing shot in a scary movie, but in this moment it felt serene. The mountains in the distance were almost completely dark save for a few stray lights, but they weren't imposing or intimidating. It was rare to find such a large, uninhabited area in the city, and that made it feel even more special.

Looking down on the house across the street, windows blackened as the married couple and their two-year-old daughter slept inside, a calming peace washed over me that I'd never felt before. Even with my relapse last night, maybe there was still hope I could find someone who made me feel as grounded as I did staring out those windows. Maybe, in spite of last night, I could still change the patterns of guilt and shame that led me to every bad decision. Maybe this was my first step, buying this house. Not just a house to get me out of apartments, which I despised living in. But a house to get me out of myself, out of my routine of anxiety and self-involvement, to evolve into the person I'm meant to become. A person who doesn't self-sabotage good relationships and demonize any kind of opposition. The type of person who can keep good people around him, and has people to come home to. A person who has a home.

My zen moment was rudely interrupted by a Miley-sized wrecking ball-type wallop to my lower spine with what I can only imagine was a sledgehammer. It knocked the wind immediately out of me and sent me to my knees. Embarrassingly the first thought I had—other than ouch—was I hope this doesn't ruin my kimono. It tears incredibly easily and was such a pain to order from China. With the prevalence of ecommerce, you'd think they'd have it down to a science, but this particular site had so many hoops to jump through, I felt like a circus performer. And after being bludgeoned in the back I'd be lucky to do step aerobics again, let alone jump.

As I blinked rapidly to clear my vision, I began crawling toward the stairs. It is so pathetic to admit that I crawled. What's more degrading than reducing a person to a movement he grew out of during infancy? Nevertheless, I crawled to the stairs and threw myself down them in a dismal attempt to get away, disregarding my well-thought-out escape plan. I should have taken a sharp right at the top of the stairs into the den, where I could've locked the door behind me and climbed out the window to make the short drop a story and half to the ground. Even if I'd injured myself in the fall, I could've easily hobbled to the neighbor's side door.

No, instead of following my carefully constructed road to safety, I made my fourth brilliant move in disgracefully tumbling down the short flight of stairs into the living room. My back was throbbing and my vision wasn't quite steady, but I still managed to pitifully stagger to my feet using the wall as a temporary crutch. My heart was racing faster than the time I was talked into Barry's Bootcamp. That hyper-acceleration was a combination of exhaustion and pure hatred for Dacoda, the steroid-inflated instructor screaming what a wimp I was for not curling with heavier weights. If I'd had the energy I would've beaten him with that ten-pounder and shown him just how heavy it could be.

But now the rapidity of my heartbeat and breath weren't the result of an overpriced and overhyped workout, but of the sheer terror of living through my first true home invasion. Prior to this moment, I would've hoped to stay level-headed and collected in a moment of crisis. In practice I froze faster than Elsa. My brain completely stopped processing. I tried to remember what route I'd planned from here—did I try to make it out through the sliding glass doors to the balcony? or was I supposed to continue even further down the stairs at the opposite end of the room to the garage?

As I stood like a toddler trying to solve a Rubik's Cube, a hand palmed the back of my head and thrust it into the glass door. In movies they always tell us that one great exertion of force will send a body crashing through any pane of glass. In real life, that's not the case. My face was thrust into the glass, but it mocked said thrust by staying fully intact and instead breaking my nose. My assailant didn't let this dissuade him though, oh no. He took it as a sign to persist, and this time persevered with an even stronger push that sent me shattering through onto the balcony. My fifth mistake in this wonderful outing was the total lack of any action due to my preoccupation with how closely life was emulating Sarah Michelle Gellar's death scene in *Scream 2* (spoiler alert). Had I not been in searing pain from the broken nose and thousands of tiny glass shards tearing at my entire body, I may have even giggled.

With barely enough time for the air to chill my skin, a pair of hands grabbed me at the ribs and tossed me into the air like a rag doll. Time moved in slow motion: as I rotated like an ice dancer nailing a triple Lutz, I noticed every leaf on every branch of every tree surrounding my house. I caught a glimpse of the roof—had it always been flat on top? How is that possible when the ceiling is vaulted inside in the living room? Along the descent I realized there were no rain gutters, which I assumed came standard on any home purchase. While careening past the balcony, I made my sixth and final grave error of the night: rather than take a long hard stare at my attacker, noting every wrinkle and probably recognizing the steely cold eyes staring back, I searched the exterior of my home for additional annoyances. Not that knowing who brutalized me would change the outcome, but at least I could've shouted "Lee Harvey Oswald!" or "O.J. Simpson!" so there would be no debate during the trial. But alas, I could only think about how unsafe those tiny two-by-fours were that held up the balcony as I plummeted to the cement, cracking my skull open and spilling what little brains I had onto the street.

I've accepted that I'm probably dying. I'm not happy about it, nor the circumstances in which it has occurred. I deserve better. I should've been shot so I can say I had no way of defending myself, or at least had a gang of surly thugs team up on me so I can look back and feel good about my attempt at fighting them off. I should be fully clothed, preferably in an outfit that would make people say, "It's so sad to lose such a handsome fella". I shouldn't have ruined my favorite kimono by having it crumpled beneath me getting irrevocably stained with the blood seeping from my body. I should've worked out tonight instead of having my third cheat meal of the week. I should've had someone to look after me other than Stanley Kowalski.

My vision is starting to go dark. There's a lot of black surrounding a tiny pinhole of a sightline. Stanley Kowalksi's still on the railing, looking down and either waiting for me to get up or finally feeling superior to me. Most likely the latter, because he only waits for me when it's time to be fed, and he's already eaten tonight. The figure emerges from inside and stands behind Stanley Kowalski for a moment, then gives him a swift shove over the edge. He screeches all the way down until I hear the soft patter of his paws on concrete. At least he can land on all fours.

I really wish I hadn't eaten pasta for dinner.

THE BEST FRIEND

The worst part about a lesbian bar is all the dudes that show up. Gay or straight, they're all obnoxious. Gay dudes think it's a pissing contest to prove they're the fun homosexuals, so try to center the bar around themselves. And straight dudes think it's a bacchanal of ravenous women awaiting the perfect dick, which just so happens to be theirs. Note to straight dudes: your dick is not perfect. Even if you are blessed with that magically stupendous, jaw-dropping deity of a penis—we're not interested.

This particular Friday night five years ago was no exception. I sauntered into Truck Stop, the ladies night at Here Lounge (whose name I'm sure was the result of some arrogant owners wanting to ridicule drunken conversations. Example: Friend 1: "Just got to the club, where are you?" Friend 2: "Here." "Where? I don't see you." "I'm at Here." "In the front or back?" "No, I'm AT Here." "I heard you, but I don't see you. Put your hand up or something." "I'm at Here *Bar*." "Oh. This was stupid.") The whole bar itself was pretty much a mess. The half outdoor/half indoor spacing of it sounds like a good idea in theory, but in practice it's divisive and makes the space feel smaller. When you walk in, you're presented with a fork-in-the-road decision—go left to stay outside amongst the limited seated and sparse trees escorting you along, or to the right to stay inside the structure where there's an immediate bar and some "VIP" booths (some real LA douchery). And all the way in the back is another giant bar and what they claim to be a dancefloor, but in actuality is no bigger than a walk-in closet (so I hear— I've never actually had a walk-in closet). But their lesbian night was pretty decent, mostly because Los Angeles has no lesbian scene. Literally. The only other lesbian bar was The Palms and it closed about a year after I moved here. Here as in Los Angeles, not the bar.

By the time I pulled up, every lesbian was already crammed in there (Here). Normally the night ends up this way, but I always go on the earlier side to claim my spot at the bar so I don't have to elbow my way through a mass of dykes to get a drink. This particular night I was running late due to the asshole who rear-ended me at a stop sign on my way home from work and decided to drive off. I tried to snap a picture of his license plate with my phone but was too busy cursing him to keep it steady. And there's no possibility of identifying a black Prius in this city, so I was left to deal with the damages on my own (Prius drivers are the worst FYI, they're all assholes).

I sneered at the prospect of being woman-handled through this crowd, but what else was I going to do on a Friday night? I gave myself a pass on weeknights for watching *Scandal* on my own with a glass of wine, but as a single woman I wasn't giving up on the weekends just yet. As I turned sideways to squeeze through a narrow canal separating a trio of hipsters and a quartet of over-styled femmes discussing clean beauty brands ("our skin is the biggest organ on our bodies and every day we're covering it with all these toxic chemicals. We have to hold these companies responsible"), a hand grasped my shoulder. I turned and there she was—Velociraptor. Nicknamed such because she kept her pedicured toenails long, which I find disgusting. She also shared the same murderous glare, at least in this moment.

"You never called me back." Her palm was light on my shoulder but her fingertips dug into me as if to warn that she could hold this death grip forever. She used her claws like a raptor too.

I didn't know how to respond, because I had in fact not called her back after the discovery of her talons killed our relationship before it began. I couldn't tell her the truth though, because how crazy would that sound? All I came up with was, "Yeah I did."

Fury raged deep within her and seeped through her eyes, the right one expanding wide and the left squeezing into a slit that twitched uncontrollably. Her mouth opened then shut in a battle between her expletives and self-control. I unintentionally scowled as I tried to free myself from her grasp, terrified of what might spew forth. I don't have a great poker face so I'm sure she could read the terror/disgust in my expression. Part of me wondered if, like a Velociraptor, she would use her elongated claws as a weapon on me. If so, that would not only be painful but vomitous.

"Ladies on ladies on ladies! This shit is my dream. I'm gonna colonize this place like Columbus."

Enter The Straight Douche. Had my right arm not been debilitated by the razor nails digging into my shoulder, I would've clubbed his Neanderthal ass. On the plus side, this seemed to distract Velociraptor's hatred from me.

"Don't be a pig Brody."

Of course his name was Brody. If you want to ensure your over-privileged child turns into the king of all d-bags, name him Brody.

Her side-eye toward him contained the same venom that was directed at me, though her grip didn't let up. "Plus Columbus didn't colonize anything. He infected an entire population then raped, pillaged and robbed them of everything they owned."

His gaze settled on me and the idiotic wheels turned slowly in his brain until realization came through. "Did you hit that? Hot." I could tell Velociraptor had the same impulse to slaughter him that I did.

"Shut the fuck up, Brody." She released me so she could hit him repeatedly. His stupid face was a mixture of horror and shock at the outburst.

"What?"

"I told your mom if you were going to visit for spring break, you couldn't be a prick."

I was shocked that Velociraptor could know or possibly be related to this bag of dicks, but rather than dwell on it, I took the opportunity to make a swift exit straight to the back bar. It was like Frogger trying to maneuver through the masses. I moved quickly and lithely without looking back, for fear Velociraptor might still be hunting me. Despite my size I'm pretty elegant when scurrying through a crowd. One nerdy lesbian sneered when I accidentally stepped on her imitation brogue, but I was gone before she could make her snarky comment. When I finally reached the bar, I had to muscle my way up to the front, which for me is not too difficult since I'm generally larger than most women and know how to throw my weight around. When I finally made it, I bumped into someone who, when I looked up, I discovered was not an attractive female for me to flirt with but yet another dude. I rolled my eyes at the testosterone.

"Oh no, don't mind me. I wasn't just standing here."

"Uh, look around. This bar is meant for me, not you."

"Whatever." He had a shot in his hand and promptly downed it. He tossed it back on the bar where it clinked into another shot glass, which I can only presume was also his. This was my intro to Damien.

I inched slightly away from him and leaned over the bar in a feeble attempt to catch the bartender's attention. They always seem to ignore me. Some friends tell me I'm paranoid, but once you've watched a line of people at every bar get served before you, you start to take it personally. Under my breath (or so I thought) I mumbled, "Who do you have to blow to get some pussy around here?"

"I know *Kissing Jessica Stein*." I turned my head slightly to see Damien looking down at a shot in front of him.

"Good, you should." He swallowed the shot immediately. "How did you get another drink already?"

He pointed to his left, the opposite direction of me. "Bartender." Another wannabe-actress-bartender was fluttering to every other person waiting for a drink except me.

"Goddammit." I hate LA bartenders. Even in a girl bar, a moderately attractive white dude gets served before I do. Granted, I'm probably not the best judge of how attractive a guy is, but I'd say he's a solid 6.5 to 7. He was a slight guy who looked more like a boy, his face reading about five years younger than his actual age. Meaning at best he looked like a high school graduate, and at worst a close friend of Michael Jackson. He shot me a quick smile and there was something about the curve of his mouth that was suspicious, like he was a lion convincing a lamb they're friends right before he slaughters it. And yet he was dressed in clothes a bumpkin fresh from the corn fields would buy his youngest son because he thought they were hilarious. His brightly colored t-shirt probably came from the children's department at Target.

"Nice shirt."

"Thanks. I got it at Target."

"I was being sarcastic."

"I wasn't."

I turned back to the bar and searched for anyone who might be able to serve me some alcohol. Noticing my complete failure, he slid a shot in front of me.

"How do you keep getting more?" He shrugged and raised his new glass to toast. "What is it?"

"It's your birthday present, fuckhead. Open it. Or...drink it."

"Oh you think I don't know Courtney Love?" I raised my tiny glass to his sightline. "I can't just leave—the bartender." I threw back what turned out to be tequila, which was good luck for me. Had it been say, Jäger, this would be a much different story. Damien grinned at my knowledge of his quote and matched my swig.

"I think I'm just gonna go home and kill myself. Want to share a cab?"

"Do you want to make slow passionate love, or should I keep the meter running?"

"These matches are disappointing me!"

"Fuck you motherfuckers." I feigned throwing a drink at the television to highlight the moment.

"You could stand naked with a mattress strapped to your back and still look like a vestal virgin."

"Do you think that'd work?"

Our first of many recitations of movie quotes was stopped short by the pervy lech who snaked up behind Damien out of nowhere. He was suddenly leaning on the bar so close to him that his toned arm was basically around his waist. He laughed stupidly to interject himself into our conversation.

"What are you guys talking about?"

Damien side-eyed him dismissively. "*200 Cigarettes*. Above your pay grade."

"Oh you smoke? I'd love a ciggie." He wasn't bright but he was shiny. Even this dim lighting was reflecting off his overly-Botoxed and chemically peeled face.

"It's a movie." I don't know why I felt the need to share that, but instantly regretted it.

Muscle Botox kept his stupid smirk directed at Damien and leaned in closer. "I like movies." He waited for one of us to react. We didn't. "Do you like scary movies?"

Damien didn't seem impressed with the forced perfection creeping closer to him. He kept his body facing me. "Nice one. Keep trying."

"What's your favorite scary movie?"

At this Damien turned to face him. "So either you're a creepy stalker who's figured out the best way to hit on me is through scary movie quotes, or you're an actual serial killer prepping me for my murder. Either way, it's not coming off well for you."

"What're you talking about?" Muscle Botox didn't seem to understand the game he was playing. He wasn't even in the same sport.

"Run along Billy. Dial someone else."

Muscle Botox looked to me as if I would help him. I stared blankly and he pushed off the bar in a huff, but not before muttering, "Who's Billy? My name's Christian, asshole."

Damien turned back to me and we both smiled. "I mean, it is kinda my dream to have a guy pick me up with quotes from *Scream*, but he smelled like he walked through Nordstrom and sprayed himself with all the free cologne testers. What's he gonna do for our first date, take me to dinner on the free samples at Costco?"

Without me even realizing, Damien once again magically procured another round of shots. I was both annoyed at his out-doing of me and concerned at how quickly we were assaulting our livers.

"Seriously? More?"

"We're drinking our feelings."

"What're we feeling?"

"Drunk." I couldn't argue with that, so we both downed them. Damien swayed a little after setting his glass down. "We should be friends."

"Should we? Why?"

"Because we clearly like the same movies. Because most people in LA suck, and I can tell that you don't. And I'm really funny, and I'd like to see if you are too."

He was right about one thing—most people in LA do suck. It's as if they see someone running down the street and assume there's a race going on, so have to join in because they're desperate to win. Emphasis on desperate. And there I am standing on the sidelines, asking everyone what the prize is but no one has any idea. So I end up handing out water, hoping one day someone will include me.

Before I had the chance to agree (or disagree), the onslaught of alcohol caused Damien to lose his legs. I caught his arm before he completely collapsed.

"Oh you need to go."

"No you off don't I walk this—" He instantly became a sorority girl revenge drinking her way through a breakup. I crouched down a little to slide my shoulder under his armpit and maneuvered him toward the exit.

"If you puke on my shoes you're buying me new ones." They weren't that nice, but if he'd ruined them I would've told him they're from Maxfield. He mumbled some more gibberish that I took to be defiant, but he didn't have the capacity to physically protest so it didn't matter.

Out on the curb, I propped him up against a light pole. "Where do you live?" His response was a grunt followed by some drool that made an unexpectedly quick exit from his mouth. I later learned this was his pre-puke ritual.

As I considered how much longer I wanted to entertain this charity case, I scanned the area for anything that might give me an out without feeling like a total asshole. Inadvertently I found myself staring back at the bar's interior, my eyes stupidly focused on the exact spot where Velociraptor continued her pursuit. We locked in. I could tell she was ready to pounce, her protruding eyes indicating I had little time to save myself. I had to move fast.

"Back to my place I guess."

Damien listlessly tried to swat at me as I tried to grab him, but only managed to almost knock himself over. Luckily for him, I have great reflexes and caught him before he fell. One of the bouncers at the club stepped toward us as I propped him back up against the pole.

"You can't stand here."

Damien doesn't like being told what he can or especially what he can't do, and his anger allowed him to actually find somewhat coherent words. "I pay my taxes. This is my sidewalk, I can stand where I want." To emphasize his point, he lost his balance.

The bouncer ignored him and looked to me. "Get him out of here."

"We're going."

I dragged Damien to one of the cabs waiting outside capital H Here and poured him into the backseat. He immediately laid down so I had to push his surprisingly firm ass to make an inch for myself. Looking at Damien you'd think he'd have a bony ass, but underneath those faded GAP jeans he's got some junk in his trunk. For a white boy at least.

When we finally got to my place I paid the driver and half-helped half-dragged Damien from the car up the path to my porch. Even in his stupor, I could tell he was judging my garden apartment, his bleary eyes scanning back and forth as he tried to walk. He mumbled something that I know was meant to be sassy, to which I retorted, "I know, my place is way cute." He responded by spitting out some more pre-vomit. "Watch the foliage, I just planted those." I hadn't, the owners lined both sides of the path with an arid desert landscape filled with a variety of succulents long before I moved in. But Damien didn't need to know that.

I pulled the screen open to my yellow painted door and fumbled to get the keys out of my pocket while balancing Damien. I'm a responsible renter and also paranoid about break-ins, so I always keep my door locked. I live by myself and love a good cop drama (yay *CSI*), so have seen way too many single-woman-stalked storylines to haunt me. In the very difficult process of single-handedly pulling the keys from my pocket, I lost my hold on Damien and he lurched backward with no ability to catch or brace himself. Thankfully I caught him before tragedy (or concrete) hit. All he could do was laugh as I yanked the keys from my left pocket and opened the door.

I briskly escorted him inside and took him directly to the bathroom. I don't know if his sober time was up or his body instinctively knew where it was, but he immediately hurled up what seemed like every ounce of fluid, food and bodily organ contained within him. His head remained plunged in the toilet bowl for an excessive amount of time, and when he was finally capable of catching his breath, he looked up to see me sitting cross-legged on the floor beside him. He was oblivious to my presence up to that moment.

"I think I'm dying."

"So you should drink some water."

I had a glass on the floor at my feet and slid it an inch closer to him. He clutched it with shaking hands and took a sip. I watched him swallow the cold water, but before it could hit his stomach it regurgitated right out. His head immediately shifted back to the toilet bowl and spewed everything from inside. He coughed twice into the bowl before raising his head. Needless to say he looked like shit.

"Do you want some toast?" He moaned, his eyes a thin slit as he could barely open them. "It'll help soak up the alcohol."

I don't know if that's actually true or not, but anyone who's ever handled a drunkard has said that. It seems accurate.

"I think I have alcohol poisoning," he managed to stumble out.

"Oh ok, you're the drama type. I see you." I got up off the floor. "I'm going to bed then."

"I'm serious."

"Everyone who's drank too much thinks they have alcohol poisoning. You'll be fine." I started walking out of the bathroom to my room when he made a sound like a baby elephant being separated from its mother. I didn't stop but shouted over my shoulder, "The only thing you have is puke on your face, you should wipe yourself off. And drink more water, you need to hydrate." He curled up on the floor by the toilet and I turned the light off, feeling like a mother putting her drunk baby in the crib. Men are, and always will be, children.

In retrospect, there's a strong possibility that Damien actually did have alcohol poisoning and should've gone to a hospital. My weak attempt at maternal nurturing really should've been replaced with an IV of fluids. I heard him puking on and off for most of the night, and all I did was silently grumble to myself about being woken up. In my defense, I'd only known him a few hours and didn't feel obligated to him. Yet.

The next morning, I awoke in bed to the sound of the TV blaring. The voices of elderly men bickering and a canned laugh track emanated through the walls, so either I brought us back to a nursing home accidentally, or Damien had odd taste in sitcoms. I slumbered out of bed to investigate.

"Shouldn't you have the volume down low with that kind of hangover?" I questioned from the doorway.

"The noise distracts me from the throbbing pain shooting through my body." He was laid out on the couch in a semi-fetal position. His head didn't turn away from the TV as he responded.

"Are you watching *Frasier*?"

"Sure am."

"Why?"

"It's comforting. And I had a sex dream about him in college once."

"Really didn't need to know that."

"He's a really good lay."

"Please stop talking." I started toward the kitchen in an attempt to stop the conversation and find some food. "Also that was dream Frasier, of course he's going to be good. You don't know about real life Frasier."

"He's good in real life too. You can tell."

"How? No, I don't want to know."

"There's a look. You can see it in the eyes."

"Wait, wasn't he married to that Housewife who threw her fake leg across the table?"

"Nope, that was some other faux-rich lunatic."

"Ah. Then I would've believed he was good in real life. If you marry a chick like that you're into some kinky shit."

I'd made it to the kitchen and was searching through the fridge and cabinets for something to eat. I'm always starving first thing when I wake up. Even if I eat right before I go to bed, my body needs immediate sustenance in the morning. I'll have some pretty fucked up dreams too. This one time I ate buffalo wings and creamed spinach from Baby Blues around ten pm and dreamt that my cousins and I were being held hostage in the basement of some old castle by Nazis wearing neon blue uniforms. There was some kind of Nazi convention going on down the hall. It was very uncomfortable, but also gave me some good style inspo.

Sadly for me, despite knowing that I'll always be hungry first thing when I wake up, I never have food in the house. I closed all the cabinets loudly in frustration, not wanting to slam them like a child, but not adult enough to keep from reacting.

"There's nothing to eat in the house. We should go get something."

"I'm half past dead, there's no way I'm moving off this couch for at least a day. But if you're going out, will you grab me something too? Nothing too heavy though, just a banana or something."

"Excuse me? When did I become your Florence Nightingale?"

"I'm your guest."

"An uninvited one."

"I didn't ask to come here, so technically you kidnapped me."

"No one's holding you against your will. Please." I opened the yellow front door and ushered him out with my hand.

"Come on, please."

I shut the door quickly. "Uh-uh, don't whine. Do not. It won't get you anything but my resentment."

"Fine, but if I die it's on your conscience. And your couch."

I rolled my eyes in resignation and stepped into my Adidas slides. "Fine. I'll be right back."

"If we were in a horror movie you'd be walking out to your death."

"If we were in a horror movie I would've been dead already."

"Sidebar—can you feed my cat while you're out? He's probably wondering where his food is."

I normally don't have anything against cats, but I have a strong opposition to people over-asking on favors. Damien was the queen of that, and he could read the discontent on my face.

"I can give you my keys and the address. It's no problem." Clearly he was illiterate. "Stanley Kowalski's really friendly."

"I'm not feeding your cat."

"Please?"

"What'd I say about whining."

"He'll starve."

"Stop being dramatic too. I'll feed your stupid cat, but only because I like animals."

"Stanley Kowalski. He likes his full name."

"Don't push it."

I never gave in on the whole call-me-by-your-full-name thing, but I did trek all the way from my cute Sunset Junction apartment to his "WeHo-adjacent" Culver City pad. In LA time, that means I could've almost flown to Hawaii. When you look on a map, most areas of LA don't seem that far apart, but the actual journey can take a ludicrous amount of time. And it's always a journey, even without a ton of traffic. I know everyone bitches about the traffic in LA, but it's no joke. It's another of the infuriatingly shitty things about this city.

When I finally made it to his place, I was pleasantly surprised to find a parking spot right out front (add parking to the shit list). I like to think the universe was thanking me for my act of kind generosity. His building looked like one of those Golden Era Hollywood complexes. It had a French chateau style to it, with cylindrical turrets on each of the corners that came to a point and look like a flag should be raised atop, like Cinderella's castle. The red awning that welcomed you into the white plastered building seemed much too fancy for Damien. Considering he spent the night on my tiled floor in front of a toilet, most things seemed too fancy for Damien.

But then the interior didn't hold up to what the exterior was selling (which can be said of most people, places and things in LA), so it all made sense. The carpet in the entry looked like it escaped a seventies lounge only to get interred at a nineties retirement community. Cheap mirrors were peeling off the walls around the sole elevator pathed directly in front of me. This felt right for him.

When I opened the door to his apartment on the third floor, Stanley was seated five feet in and staring directly at me. I don't know how but he knew I was coming, and over the course of my friendship with Damien, I learned that Stanley always knew when someone was coming. He stayed perfectly silent and still as I creeped around him, and only moved to pivot his body so he could watch as I poured food into his bowl in the kitchen. He didn't even come in to get the food while I was there. He remained in that same spot as I walked back to the door and only pivoted again to watch me leave. When I closed the door and locked it, I realized I'd been holding my breath the entire time I was in there. Stanley's intense.

When I got back I found Damien staring at a rerun of *Wheel of Fortune* on the Game Show Network, which I later found out he was addicted to. I didn't even know I had the Game Show Network; I don't really like game shows so it's no use to me. In this episode, no one could figure out the Before and After of LADIES WHO LUNCH BOX despite only missing the O's and the U. People are so dumb sometimes and I really can't take it.

"Thanks for feeding Stanley Kowalski."

"Your cat's weird."

"He warms up once you get to know him." He didn't.

I sat down next to him on the couch, watching in awe as contestants fumbled through wrong answers. "Why are you watching this?"

"Oh it's the best. People are so stupid, it feeds my superiority complex. What'd you get to eat?"

"Macaroni and cheese. I don't even care if you don't like it, it's my jam so you'll just have to deal."

"If I had any will to move right now, I'd hug you so hard."

"Feeling like more than just a banana I take it?"

"I'm kinda starving."

"Fine." I pushed myself off the couch—it's really deep and soft, it's the best for passing out watching TV—and busted out my trusty pot in the kitchen. I really don't care if anyone else likes it, cause I know there's a lot of judgment against boxed mac 'n' cheese, but I love that shit.

"Please tell me you got Kraft and not Velveeta."

I almost threw the pot on the floor when he asked me that. "Velveeta is disgusting and I am offended that you would even ask me that. Get out."

"We just met, I don't know your taste level yet."

"My taste level is the shit."

"I know that now, and am sorry to ask. I had to be sure. It won't happen again."

"It better not. Fucking Velveeta."

This time I did throw the pot on the stove, but only a little. It wasn't a full-fledged hammer throw, but enough to make a clang that rang throughout the apartment.

By the time I finished making our divine cuisine of powdered cheese atop elbow macaroni, *Wheel of Fortune* was wrapping up. I grabbed two forks and the pot by the handle and settled back into the couch next to

Damien. I set the pot between us and handed him a fork as he started flipping through channels.

"Such service."

"This is a fancy establishment." I punctuated by stabbing a few macaroni hard. "You're gonna have to sit up, you know."

"I'm hoping the universe will just put the macaroni in my mouth."

"Lemme know how that goes for you," I said with a mouthful.

He slowly raised himself up while groaning pathetically (I told you, dramatic), and with a limp arm basically threw his fork into the pot. He shook his hand as he brought the food nearer his lips, finally snapping his mouth closed over it like an amnesiac re-learning how to function. All I could do was watch, which I'm pretty sure was his intention anyway.

"So no *Jeopardy*?"

"Hard pass. I don't need to feel dumber than I already am."

"Gimme the remote, I'll choose something."

He looked me in the eye as he slowly handed it over. "This is a big test right now."

"I know."

"This is going to determine the future of our friendship."

"And not just for me. You might fail too."

"Fair."

"Actually you know what, no." I got up and opened the doors to my TV stand where I kept all my DVDs (yes I had a DVD collection and still do, it's massive and awesome). "We're gonna have a real test." I pulled out one of my favorites.

"Oooh, what is it?"

"A movie by someone you definitely know, but not one that most people talk about."

"I like the sound of this."

I popped it in the player, pushed the drive shut and slid back to the couch. "Now if you know this, we're good."

"And if I don't?"

"Strike one."

The movie started playing and I side-eyed him to catch his reaction. Once the seventies music started his brow furrowed, but when the Miramax logo came on his mouth opened in recognition.

"Is this...?"

"Boo-yah!"

"I love this movie!"

"*Jackie Brown*. When you absolutely, positively have to kill every last motherfucker in the room, accept no substitutes."

"Is it this aisle Louis? Is it? Louis? Louisssssss? Is it this aisle or the next one?"

"She's so annoying, she deserved to get shot."

"When the woman sings 'Baby Love' to Robert De Niro, I love that."

"Of course you do. You probably want her outfit."

"Duh. And Robert Forster is so charming, I have a little crush on him in this."

"Uh, Pam Grier? She's the crush."

"Oh that goes without saying. But I might want to be her more than be with her."

"I'll give you that."

"So we both pass the test I guess."

"I guess so. This is the start of a beautiful friendship."

"Weirdly I've never seen that."

"Funny, neither have I."

A few hours later after finishing watching (and re-enacting) *Jackie Brown*, Damien managed to drag himself from my couch to shower at his own place. I'm pretty sure he called me the second he was done.

"So I'm kinda bored, want to order food and watch another movie?"

I too was kinda bored since he'd left, so I was on board. "Yeah sure. Wanna come here again? Your cat kinda freaks me out."

"Stanley Kowalski."

"Whatever, Stanley."

"Yeah sure, I can come there. But you're gonna have to make friends with him at some point." I never really did, but I told Damien I'd at least try (which I didn't really).

We watched *Josie and the Pussycats* with Rosario Dawson and Tara Reid that night because we couldn't believe we'd both actually seen it before. It's one of the best good bad movies, a genre we both seemed to have an affinity for, and when we watched those together, it made them even better. I couldn't even get anyone to consider going to that movie with me (at the time I had a thing for Rosario, I got over it once she shat on *Rent*—well, Chris Columbus is mostly responsible but she was still party to it), let alone find someone who would laugh at Parker Posey's surprise lisp with me.

We spent almost every day together after that, and four months later we moved in with each other. It wasn't much of a stretch at that point. One of us was always sleeping at the other's house, though that first night was the only time he slept on my couch. He started in on some drawn out (whiny) story of the couch causing the vertebrae in his spine to shift and he hadn't found a good chiropractor in LA when I gave in. I didn't care anyway—what was he gonna do, make a move on me? Even if he wasn't super into the d, I could take him any day. For my part, I refused to allow Stanley to sleep in bed when I crashed at his (don't for a second think I was about to sleep on a couch).

Surprisingly (to me at least), it was my idea that we move in together. I was making him watch *Set It Off* cause he'd never seen it when it occurred to me.

"We should move in together."

"Ok."

"Wanna start looking this weekend?"

"Sure."

Another trait we shared: our decision making is pretty quick.

The first place we saw was a two bedroom garden apartment on San Vicente just north of Beverly. Tucked in the back of a hedged-in former single family home now (semi-illegally?) split into separate apartments, it had a quaint little orange tree outside the bathroom window and a wall of jasmine closing in a tiny patio. We both loved it and magically we got it. That's unheard of in LA—no one gets the first apartment they love. Before I found my Sunset Junction place, I was looking for three months after my initial apartment turned out to be a dump and possible meth den. Once again the universe was smiling down on us.

We moved in two weeks after we first stepped foot into the apartment. I broke my lease with a sob story of my sick aunt in Chicago who doesn't exist; Damien told his landlord he had his heart broken and needed to find himself. He brought Stanley and we quickly developed an understanding. I left him alone and he didn't shit on my bed. It was a real concern. One time Damien and I had sushi at this really good, kinda divey joint in a strip mall around the corner from my Sunset Junction place (which closed not too long after I moved sadly), and decided to get a drink at Akbar after. Akbar's the "hetero friendly" gay bar on the east side—I don't think we need to pander to the straight folks since every bar on the planet is hetero friendly, but it's got a cool vibe so I'm not mad at it. But he didn't get home to feed Stanley until like eleven or midnight and Stanley'd taken a huge dump on the bed right where Damien always slept. That cat does not fuck around, but neither do I.

In retrospect, I'm shocked that I moved in with someone I'd only known for a few months. It very easily could've gone epically wrong. But in the moment it didn't feel so reckless, it just felt natural. And I guess that's why it worked; we both could tell we shared a similar mentality. The same little things annoy us both, like people who don't squeeze the toothpaste from the top down and leave the tube all smashed up. It's not difficult people, roll it if you have to. And leaving dirty dishes all over the house. That's just disgusting. I don't care where you eat, I love eating on the couch while watching TV so am not particular about that. But take your goddamn dish to the kitchen and rinse it off when you're done. Why would I want to scrape crusty food off a plate that's been sitting in your room for days?

Damien had a roommate who used to do that and it drove him crazy. He said one time he just collected all the dirty dishes from around the house and left them in the roommate's bedroom. Apparently it backfired cause the roommate just ignored them and Damien ended up washing them all anyway.

The whole time we lived together it was like we were in a relationship. I don't mean that in a creepy way; every friendship is a relationship anyway. But it was like it was just the two of us. I think we clicked so hard and living together made it so easy. Damien said to me once after an attempt at a date that he left halfway through cause the guy was super lame, and he'd rather be sitting on the couch with me. We just got each other, so we spent all our time together.

We were going out a lot then, hitting up the gay bars on the boulevard. I was PA-ing at the time, mostly on commercial shoots so it didn't matter if I was hungover (which was pretty much every day). I first moved out here cause I thought I wanted to be a producer, but that life fucking sucks I gotta say. I know I didn't work on anything big, but even on the shit ones I was doing the people were nuts. ADs shouting "MAKEUP" or "WARDROBE" instead of people's actual names, and everyone snorting coke in the porta-potties like it's the 80s. They all complained about never sleeping, being mal-nourished and completely alone. It was depressing, man. And Damien was striking out with his acting or writing or whatever he was trying to make happen, and working random temp jobs to make money, so he was always wanting to go out. Mostly to find a hookup and get laid, but even when he didn't, we'd bar hop until we couldn't stand up. Back then it was fun to be drunk.

I think Damien was good with our setup, having me at home and his tricks on the boulevard. Like every straight couple right? Easy burn, sorry. But even though I had fun living with him, I realized I'd isolated myself from any possibilities of finding a relationship. Not just physically too. I was comfortable in our routine of hanging out and playing his non-sexual partner. I just needed more. And not long after I had that realization, I met Lilypad.

My girlfriend doesn't know this, but I met her a little while before she thinks we had our first intro. The first time I saw her was at a Halloween screening of *Labyrinth*. Some event production company that specializes in unnecessary takeovers turned one of the theaters in downtown LA into a prom for everyone who didn't get a date for their original one. The theater itself was one of the many reno projects the city was attempting to liven up the downtown area. I have to give it to them, it was actually a pretty cool idea. Most of the theaters were probably pretty epic in their original form, but were completely decayed after decades of neglect. The carpet still felt a little dingy, but they at least cleaned it enough so it looked like a relative of its former grandeur. The chandeliers rained crystals overhead, shining bright enough to make it irrelevant whether they were replacements or vintage. The ceilings around them still had chunks missing, but the leftover scaffolding showed they're still a work in progress.

Damien dressed up as David Bowie and I went as Toby, despite his protestations to get me in Sarah's big 80s ballgown (literally never). We were waiting in the endless line for a drink, him angrily impatient that anyone would make us wait and me resigned to it as a part of my life, when the crowd moved as one entity to part right down the middle. No seriously, not even metaphorically like Moses parting the Dead Sea—it *was* Moses parting the sea of deadened hipsters in downtown LA. And Moses, in this case, was Lilypad and her entourage.

To be totally honest, my first impression was that she wasn't the stand-out of the group. I'm madly in love with her so can say that without any malintent. She was beautiful, of course, but dressed down as what I'm guessing was the Stepmother? The whole group was themed, and the guy leading the pack was obviously David Bowie, albeit a cheap and pretty underwhelming version. One person was Hoggle, one girl was a very loose interpretation of one of the Fireys by basically tar and magenta-feathering herself, and my favorite was the pocket gay dressed as the Worm. Damien's too—he embarrassingly approached him and patted him on the head while cooing. I swear Damien narrowly avoided the actual daggers being shot from his eyes.

And then there was Lilypad. She was dressed in some super basic 80s garb that was way more *Working Girl* than *Labyrinth*. Her frizzy locks were appropriately pinned up on both sides, and a swipe of green shadow was haphazardly painted across her eyelids. She had on someone's mother's closed-toed sensible heels with her legs stuffed into nude pantyhose. None of the elements went together or were particularly well done, but she didn't seem to care. She strutted with those over-the-top costumes like she was the Regina George.

After finally getting our drinks (we ordered three each so we wouldn't have to wait in line again) we slipped past all the chattering chaos to nab seats at the front of the right wing balcony. It made me feel important being up there, like I was receiving a Kennedy Center honor or something. I leaned over the balcony edge to look down upon (literally and figuratively) the plebeians below and just like any romantic comedy, there she was. Directly below us.

Firey was as obnoxious as her costume, flapping her arms and cawing like she might actually take off. Bowie was trying to hit on...a boy? Girl? It was hard to tell from high up and with the costume, but whatever person was sitting next to him, he was trying to get on them. Worm was trying to figure out how to sit in the costume, and essentially had to lay with his head on the back of the seat and his feet on the seat in front of him, the rest of his body floating. And she was on the end, sitting inconsequentially, waiting for something to begin.

I wondered if she knew the group she came with or just happened upon them (later I found out they're all really tight). She didn't appear interested in any of their doings, but wasn't bothered by them either. As if she existed in a totally different plane than they did. She didn't fidget or squirm, just sat comfortably in her skin waiting.

I must've been staring for a while because I felt Damien's massive head lean in over my shoulder. He followed my gaze.

"You're totally obsessed with her."

"I am not."

"You want to have like ten thousand of her babies."

"Shut up."

The movie began and he leaned back in his chair. Lilypad didn't move. I half watched the movie and half watched her watch the movie. I've never seen someone be so still for so long. She was either really into it or ascending to some higher level of consciousness. I know this sounds like crazy stalker talk, but the more I watched her, the more I couldn't stop watching her.

Damien leaned in again to whisper, "I gotta pee."

"Ok fine." Like I need to know his every bowel movement? He creaked out of his chair while my eyes jumped from Lilypad to the screen, just in time to see Sarah rescue Ludo. Aw, I love Ludo. Anything that blindly loyal just warms my heart.

I looked back down and—what the shit? Damien was standing next to Lilypad. Leaning over, his head next to hers. Mouth to ear? Was he talking to her? He must be talking to her. Why was he talking to her? Neither looked up at me, so hopefully he wasn't divulging my voyeuristic ways. He better not, I'd have murdered him right there.

After what felt like an exceedingly long time to be whispering to someone he'd never met, Damien finally walked away under the balcony. Lilypad never turned her head, she kept looking straight ahead at the movie the entire time. I gripped the armrests of my chair like I was trying to squeeze juice out of a lemon that would save someone's life. Damien finally sat nonchalantly next to me and acted like he was just going to resume watching this movie.

"Excuse me."

"What?"

"WHAT? You know exactly what."

"Shh, I'm trying to watch the movie."

"What did you say to her?"

"To who?"

"Jennifer Connelly. Who do you think?"

"Nothing. Be quiet, we're missing the movie."

"You missed a large part of the movie while talking to her. What did you say?"

"Shh."

"I'm not letting this go until you tell me."

The middle-aged woman behind me leaned in close, the vapors of her breath announcing her presence. "You're disrupting the movie."

"Lady, I will throw you over this balcony."

Damien turned quickly, aghast. The woman's male companion didn't take to it very well either.

"Hey that's uncalled for."

"Shut the fuck up." To my, and everyone's, surprise my voice was getting louder.

Damien put his hand on my arm. "You're making a scene."

At the same time the male companion leaned in close and asked, "What's your problem?"

I don't often get angry or threatened, but in that moment I felt both. Angry at the obvious, Damien and his stupid interjection; threatened by these two men who were getting intensely intimate in my personal space in an attempt to quiet me. I leapt to my feet and did the opposite.

"My problem is you and your cow butting into our conversation." It might've been the adrenaline but I really think I echoed through the entire theater.

What I remember next is a little blurry, probably a result of the adrenaline. Damien dragged me out of the balcony as the male companion and his lady (she wasn't a cow, I feel bad about my woman-on-woman crime) trading nasty shouts as I was pulled away. I didn't catch if any of the commotion broke Lilypad's stare, but even so she couldn't have registered it was me. I didn't even recognize myself in that moment.

Out on the street, I was weirdly out of breath. Throwing such a fit takes a lot of energy.

Damien looked up and down the street for something. "Do you think there's a bar nearby?"

"I'm sure there are plenty."

"One that we'd want to go to. I need a drink but not at some lumber-bro place."

"I don't come downtown."

"Clearly. It brings out the rage in you."

"You started it. And you still haven't told me what you said to her."

"Mature." He started walking to I don't know where, so I had to follow. "Did you bring your ID? You look even more like a child in that onesie so you're definitely getting carded."

I straightened my bright red onesie in mild offense. He was right, I was costumed as a child from a movie so really gave off an immature vibe, but I wasn't going to let him knock my look. "I don't think I need another drink."

"Of course you do. You just accosted a random couple in front of a crowded theater and the girl you're into. That's the definition of needing another drink."

"It wasn't that bad, was it?"

"We each left a full drink behind. It was bad."

I shuffled beside him feeling like crap. In that moment I thought I'd never see that beautiful mystery again. Her last impression of me would be some fitful lunatic having her *Jerry Maguire* breakdown. Thankfully, though I didn't know it in that moment, I'd have another chance with Lilypad.

It was seventeen days later, to be exact. My guilt lasted two days after *Labyrinth* and then I let it go. Honestly, Damien dragged me into watching *One Tree Hill.* I was mostly against watching those idiotic teen dramas, but I got so wrapped up in their silly lives I basically moved to Tree Hill. When are Lucas and Nathan gonna stop fighting over Haley???

On one of my very few self-imposed *OTH* breaks I made a coffee run to my local Coffee Bean and Tea Leaf. It felt less big business than Starbucks to me, despite there being a Coffee Bean within a block of every Starbucks location. I'd ordered my White Chocolate Ice Blended with almond milk and whipped cream (don't judge, it's delicious), with Damien texting me *OTH* gossip ("Slutty Rachel=teen pregnancy PSA"), when I heard a soft voice order a White Chocolate Ice Blended with almond milk and whipped cream. I looked up and there she was, her curly mahogany hair draped effortlessly over her shoulders, a vintage broche-type accessory clipped in just above her ear. When the barista asked the name she leaned in to say, "Lily, like lily pad."

She came to stand next to me in the designated "wait for your order" area. I was sweating. A lot.

"You like the white chocolate too?" I couldn't believe I got it out.

She turned so her eyes bore into mine. They're a soft blue with a hint of green around the edges, and they're mesmerizing. She could've asked me to chop off my hand and I would've done it without a thought.

"It's really good. Everyone makes fun of me but I can't stop."

"You shouldn't, it's the best."

"Plus I hate the taste of coffee but can't function without it."

"Me too! Plus, I mean, sugar."

She laughed, probably as a social courtesy, but I counted it as a victory.

The barista walked up with my drink and called out the name. "Valentina."

Lilypad's eyebrow cocked as she watched me grab my drink. "Valentina? What an exotic name."

"That's just what I use when I order. They usually don't mess it up."

This time she laughed for real. It was joyous.

"Smart. I don't think they've ever gotten my name right. I've gotten Lisa, Laura, Rory, Lori—"

"Oh I thought you were gonna say Rory and Lorelai. I would've been really jealous."

"Ha, I wish. I'd probably get Lane first."

"Not a bad fall back. Lane was always under-the-radar cool."

I was pleased that she caught my *Gilmore Girls* reference and ran with it. The barista came back with her drink this time, and handed it direct to her rather than calling the name.

"How close this time?"

She just laughed, turning the cup to show me. She laughed again as I read, "Lily Rad?" I laughed too.

"It's technically my name I guess. At least they got the important half right."

"You're giving them too much credit."

We walked out together, sipping our candy flavored coffee confections.

"You still haven't told me your name."

"Why, you want to ask me out on a date?"

"YOU STOLE MY *SCREAM* PICK UP!!" Damien literally screamed at me when I retold him this story.

"What?"

"That's from *Scream* and I told you it's my dream to get picked up by someone using quotes from that movie."

"I don't think she intentionally quoted it. There's a strong possibility she's never even seen *Scream*."

"Well, you can't go out with her then." Again there was no irony in his voice.

"I'm going out with her."

"I'd like to note for the record that I disapprove."

"Noted and filed."

Our first date was that same night (shove it with your lesbian jokes) and she came over to my place first. We were going out in the gayborhood so the plan was to walk from my apartment to the boulevard. Despite her punctuality, I was itching to go. Playing it cool has never been my forte so I'm really awesome at dating. Damien was settled into the couch as usual, barely turning his head when she knocked at the door.

I held my breath a second before swinging those fiberglass panels open to my destiny. "Hi." I got a 540 verbal on my SATs.

"Hey, you look great."

I'm glad she thought so; I was sweating my look the whole time I waited. After many outfit changes I landed on the same pants I wore to Coffee Bean and a plaid shirt jacket that really perked up my boobs. Damien picked it out in one of our first of many shopping trips together. Shopping's never really been my thing, but Damien found a way to make it not completely soul-crushing. It was back in the day right after we moved in together, I was unpacking and he came into my room as I was putting everything in my closet.

"Whoa, what is that?" he said as he sauntered in.

I was shaking out a navy blazer I wore all the time when I needed to be a little more dressed up than usual. "It's a blazer. Don't give me any shit about needing dresses."

"I would never. But exactly who is meant to wear that? I hope not you, because it looks like three of you can fit in there."

Truth right now, shopping for me is not the most pleasant experience. Most women's clothes, especially jackets and blazers, all have flares or frills and I refuse to put anything like that on my body. And shopping in the men's department alone is stupid uncomfortable, so I typically find the color blazer I want and get out as quickly as possible. Which is how I get stuck with clothes that look like I stole them from my big brother.

"I like the oversized look."

"You are not in Salt-N-Pepa and this is not 1993. We're fixing this. Today."

So he took me out that whole day to a bunch of places I never would've set foot in on my own. I remember him pulling this shirt jacket out for me. I didn't even know what a shirt jacket was.

"What is that?"

"Trust me, you're going to look great in it."

"Plaid's not really my thing."

"Just try it on."

"Put it back."

Always relentless, he pushed it closer to me. "Seriously it's going to look so good on you, I promise. Please?"

I grudgingly grabbed it from him. "Fine, I'll try it on."

"You have to show me too."

"You know I hate this."

"That's why I'm here! To make it better."

I wasn't convinced yet about the clothes he picked or his ability to make this experience anything but painful. After trying on that shirt jacket, I walked out of the dressing room fidgeting with it, not really sure how to wear it. The moment he saw me he jumped up in excitement.

"That's how a jacket's supposed to fit!" He rushed over to me and turned me to face the mirror, buttoning the jacket up from the bottom but leaving it open from my breasts up. "Look how good it makes your tits look."

"My tits are great, thank you."

"I know. And this shows 'em off. You look amazing."

I did look amazing. And I finally felt like I looked amazing. It was the first time since I can remember that I felt really good during a shopping experience. Every other time I felt out of place. If I was in the men's department, I was embarrassed for being there so tried to sneak in and out. If I was in the women's department, I felt excluded from my gender, having an entire department that said nothing to me. Every salesperson would try to find me something vaguely along the lines of what I was looking for, force me into it, then tell me how pretty I looked. I don't want to look "pretty"—I'm not a pretty person. Pretty is for ruffles and sundresses and rainbows. I want to look good, amazing, even great sometimes. I want to look dope and cool. I don't want to worry about what gender my clothes are, I just want to worry about finding the best outfit to make a girl go "Damn, she's hot." And Damien helped me feel that every time he took me shopping. Also note to salespeople: do not ever bring me clothing with ruffles.

The shirt jacket became my go-to for dates, not that I used it a ton. But LP was impressed by it on our first date, and her compliment made me stop sweating for a second. Unfortunately it didn't help with my game, because all I could respond with was, "Thanks, so do you."

She did look amazing though, truly. If I could do it again, I would've told her what a goddess she was on my doorstep. The front light played it up a little too, shedding this glow down on her like she was sent from the heavens. But her radiance is what made me speechless. She put on just the tiniest bit of makeup and it made her eyes pop even more than they usually do. When she looks at you, you never want her to look away. You can't help but be transfixed. Once you meet her in person, you get it.

"She's been dancing around like she has to pee for thirty-six minutes. I timed it." Damien leaned his head back over the couch to share this tidbit, his feet remaining kicked up on the coffee table. He always found his way into other people's moments.

Lilypad didn't seem to recognize him from the night of my breakdown, which I took as a win. Hoping she never would, I continued with the intro. "That's my roommate Damien. You can ignore him."

She looked at him then smirked back at me. "Ok. Hi, I guess."

"Don't keep her out too late. Curfew's at midnight."

"K bye." I closed the door and walked her out quickly.

I'd like to say that he got over that, but I'm a terrible liar. It wasn't so much a grudge he held against her, or even that he didn't like her—he just never seemed that interested in her. And she didn't try that hard to warm up to him either. She never acknowledged meeting him on *Labyrinth* night and I would never ask her about it for fear of revealing my obscene tantrum. I don't think she remembers though, cause she's not that good of a liar either.

As my dating life took off, I think it motivated Damien to grow out of his hookup phase. He was the queen of the one night stand, so in the beginning it was mostly just an array of pretty young things being escorted in and out of our place. I never minded because they mostly kept to themselves and I didn't have to worry about remembering their names. Although there was a period where a bunch of them started eating all my food, which is surprising since most of the guys Damien goes for are too insecure about their bodies to eat anything. I don't know if it's just the gays in LA or an epidemic, but there are a lot of dudes out there with some serious body dysmorphia. But that phase of healthy eaters made themselves at home in my pantry, so I had to leave a stern note on the fridge (something to the effect of, "Hey tricks of my roommate, don't touch my fucking food"). Damien later told me it was nasty, but I think he was just being overly sensitive.

Unfortunately for me, Damien's first semblance of a relationship was with the prick we shall not name. Robbie. That's his name. A dumb fucking name for an even dumber fucking person. You know when people say something's the worst because they don't like it, but you can think of a dozen things way worse? Well Robbie is the actual worst. I dare anyone to find a human being more heinous than him. He wasn't the least bit attractive—he had what looked like a permanently broken nose, one eye that I swear was higher than the other and a perpetual frown that even when he smiled looked depressing. I guess you can say he had a nice body, if you're into that. Which Damien was, fuck me gently with a chainsaw. And Robbie can't have higher than a second grade education—one time he literally asked if Halloween was October thirty-second or thirty-third. I'm not kidding.

So when Damien first met Robbie at Motherlode, I assumed he'd been drunk and didn't realize what he was doing. It was during a period where we were both out all the time but never together, and would drunk text each other around one am. Lilypad and I had been drinking at The Gold Coast, the old man gay bar where we felt safe from lecherous straight dudes and free from the loud twinks. Also they pour very strong drinks and charge like two dollars. We'd left around midnight to hookup at her place and I was brushing my teeth when Damien's text came through.

"Home? Dlunk cuming back w/ gus"

I gripped the toothbrush with my teeth and typed "At LPs".

A few seconds later I got "Scissor me timbers". He loved that joke.

I staggered home the next morning wearing Lilypad's sunglasses and a hangover headache. Needless to say I was not in the mood for bullshit and that's all Robbie was. He was splayed out on the couch in his dirty white briefs, his slack-jaw mouth gaping with drool spilling out onto the pillow. Annoyedly I let the door slam louder than I probably should've, and his eyes fluttered open. He looked directly at me then rolled over like a dog and went back to sleep. I marched straight into Damien's room.

"Why are your leftovers on the couch?"

Damien slept on his stomach and spoke more into his pillow than to me. "He drools too much."

"Yeah, now he's drooling all over the couch."

"Do we have any eggs? Could you make me a scramble?"

"Get rid of him before I wake up." I shuffled into my room and crawled into my glorious bed.

Robbie was not gone when I woke up, and stuck around for an astonishing eight months after. For a fuckboy that's a long time. And that's all he was to Damien. This one time I brought Lilypad over and he was just standing naked in the living room, I assume just after having sex with Damien. I lost my shit.

Let me rewind a second so you can get the full picture of how my shit got lost. In the beginning of our relationship, we always wound back up at Lilypad's. She lived alone so it made sense, it wasn't a conscious decision or anything. But after a while it felt like she intentionally dodged coming to mine, and admittedly I got a little sensitive about it. I've been told that I tend to avoid confrontation, so there were probably a few moments when I should've brought up my unease and chose not to. But this night I finally did. In my own way.

We were walking back from dinner at Taste on Melrose—they had their semi-annual Grilled Cheese bar which was Lilypad's favorite—and Lilypad was pushing to go back to hers again.

"I'm just saying we can spend some time at my place. I live by myself."

"We spend a lot of time at your place, what do you have against mine?"

"Nothing—"

"And why's it always about what you want?"

"It's not, what're you talking about?"

"Every time I suggest something you come up with an alternative."

"I do not."

"You did tonight. I said I wanted to lay low, order in and watch TV and you came back with your idea."

"You love the grilled cheese bar too, you were excited when I reminded you they had it."

"You still changed the plan, to what you want."

"You're over-reacting."

I hope I'm not the only person who doesn't take kindly to being told that. "Oh ok, my girlfriend out of nowhere mysteriously hates spending time at my house—"

"I don't hate—"

"Refusing to go there anymore and refusing to tell me why, but somehow I'm the one who's over-reacting?"

"I'm not refusing anything, I just made an alternate suggestion."

"Would you like to suggest any other ways I can change for you? What else do you hate about me?"

"Oh my god, I don't hate anything about you."

"Don't be shy. We're talking about it at least, so now's your chance."

It went on. Definitely not my finest moment but in the end we both apologized and ended up heading back to my apartment. Not to sound too shallow, but it felt like a victory. I know, relationships aren't contests. But aren't they a little? After a certain point every argument boils down to winning; you stop caring about what you're actually fighting for and just want to get your way. So this was a gold medal to hang in my trophy case.

And what's the first thing we see when I open the door to my apartment? Fucking Robbie buck ass naked. Had I not just gotten into a huge argument with my girlfriend about coming to my place, I might not have gotten so pissed. I had to literally bite my tongue to keep from verbally eviscerating him. Damien came out of his room almost immediately so he bore the brunt of my anger.

"Oh hey."

"Oh hey? I walk in my house and find your fuckboy naked dripping jizz all over my living room and all you can say is oh hey?"

"Don't call him a fuckboy, and this is our living room."

"I don't care, why is he naked in our living room?"

"He was just thirsty."

"He's always thirsty, he's the definition of thirsty. I'm tired of you always bringing him around and fucking him everywhere and finding him naked. It's disgusting."

"It was one time, and it was an accident. I've seen you two prance around in your underwear."

"At most we were running to the bathroom, and neither of us is a walking STD."

"Why are you always laying into him so much? What did he ever do to you?"

"He's fucking here. He's always here and he's a waste. If you want to fuck up your life and your place that's fine, but don't fuck up mine."

I dragged Lilypad into my room and slammed the door. This time I didn't care about being childish. She looked at me with her sad eyes and I knew I'd been too harsh.

"I'm sorry."

"You don't have to apologize to me."

"He had it coming."

"Let's just forget about them. Come to bed." She leaned back on the bed and gave me her best seduction smirk (which is really good, by the way). She never liked to dwell on angry moments, and that's a good balance for me. I tend to stew and overthink everything, leading to explosions like what just happened. That little flicker of her lips instantly flushed all my anger out my toes and arousal moved right in.

We got over it and reverted back to spending most of our time at

Lilypad's. Damien and I never talked about Robbie again until he told me he was ending it with him. It was a couple days after my blow up. We were sitting on the couch, just me and him, watching *Wheel of Fortune* again. It kinda became our tradition after that first day together.

"I think I have to break up with Robbie."

"You think?"

"Yeah. I don't think it's working."

"Vanna's dress is less of an understatement than that."

"I'm just really lonely."

I'd never really heard Damien be vulnerable like that so I was caught off guard. He didn't turn his head away from the TV but his voice was so small.

"I get it. But that doesn't mean you should stay with just anyone."

"I know."

I'm really not good at the sentimental moments, so I pretty much sat there quietly as I struggled internally to figure out what to say next. It never came, so we finished out the *Wheel* in silence. He broke up with Robbie pretty unceremoniously over text, which I know doesn't sound great but I can't judge cause it's totally a move I'd make. Robbie did not take it well.

The night after Damien ripped the band-aid off, Robbie showed up outside our apartment at two in the morning. I can't say for certain he was drunk, but he was drunk. I'd fallen asleep with my laptop next to me playing my *Fried Green Tomatoes* DVD when I heard his pip-squeak voice screaming from outside the window.

"I don't deserve this! I'm a good boyfriend, you need me."

I heard Damien's window open from the room next door. He didn't bother to raise his voice. "Robbie, go home. We were never even boyfriends."

"Yes we are, I love you."

"No you don't. Go home and sober up."

"Don't talk to me like that. You need me." It sounded like he was holding back sobs.

"I'm closing the window, goodbye Robbie."

"You'll regret doing this, you'll be sorry."

Damien closed his window.

Now I don't want to point fingers, and normally I'd say Robbie's too dumb to pull off anything beyond getting dressed every day. But considering everything, I'd say he looks pretty suspicious. He was so angry when they broke up, and after they broke up Damien started getting these weird calls from a blocked number. He would answer and no one would be there, just some heavy breathing which I could also interpret as sobs from a bitter idiot who had his heart broken. Granted they broke up a while ago, but I heard that Robbie "ran into" Damien a few days before the...you know. I still can't even say it. It's too unbelievable.

But that's not a coincidence, the Robbie run in. I don't know if he was still looking for a way to get back together with him or what. I tried calling Damien to check but never reached him. Robbie's petty enough to lash out since Damien's been doing so well, but the good news is if he did do it, then his idiocy extends to covering his tracks. I wouldn't be surprised if he left a note somewhere in the house.

A little while after Damien came to his senses about Robbie, Lilypad asked me to move in with her. It was tough because of course I loved her and wanted to, but I knew Damien would not take it well. He's very co-dependent, which is why I think he clung to Robbie so much. I wouldn't call him Damien's first love—god I hope he didn't think that—but even though Robbie's the dating equivalent of a dumpster fire, Damien convinced himself that he needed him. I didn't tell Lilypad about my apprehensions though; I didn't want her to feel like my hesitation was a reflection on how I saw our relationship. So I immediately agreed and we started making plans.

In retrospect, I didn't handle breaking the news to Damien very well. I thought it would've been better for him if I didn't give him too much time to wallow in the knowledge of my departure, so I told him the week I moved out. I tried to pack as much by myself as I could so I didn't attract his attention, but one afternoon Lilypad came over to help me pack the dishes. I have a lot of mugs; it's weird I know but I love them for some reason. I was wrapping the oversized green Oscar the Grouch mug Lilypad bought for me in newspaper when Damien came in the kitchen.

"Oh thank god, are we finally getting rid of those?" He always thought they were stupid. Honestly most people think they're stupid. I don't care.

"Ha yeah, it's your lucky day." I was trying to keep it light, once again showing that I'm not very good at playing it cool.

"What're you doing with them?"

"Oh you know."

"No I don't. That's why I asked."

"I'm taking them to our apartment. Lilypad and I are moving in together." I smiled my best Julia Roberts smile, which is nothing in comparison to hers.

"Oh wow. Ok. Thanks for telling me I guess. When are you guys moving?"

I flipped the hair that I don't have around, I'm not sure why. I always see women do it in movies to defuse a tense situation. But I'm not Beyoncé.

"This weekend."

"This weekend? What am I supposed to do about the rent?"

I hadn't thought of that, and I felt like shit for it. I think Lilypad felt it too and got uncomfortable, because she left the room.

"I'm so sorry, I can help pay it until you find a new roommate."

"No I don't want you to do that, that's crazy." He was also very proud and hated asking for help. "It's just so soon, I don't know what I'm going to do. A little heads up would've been nice."

"I know, I'm really sorry. I can help you find someone."

"I don't even really want a new roommate, why can't you just stay? We live so good together."

"I know—"

"It's not easy to live this good with someone you know? Living with her probably won't be this easy."

"You don't know that. I have to give it a shot."

"I know."

I could tell he was upset but didn't want to say anything. He didn't hang around much longer and Lilypad and I finished packing that day. He wasn't around the weekend we moved either. I think it was too hard for him. We didn't talk for a little bit after that. Like I said, I could tell he was upset so I knew he wasn't going to call me right away, and I wanted to give him his space.

In time he did reach out. I don't know, maybe a couple months or so. We met for dinners and caught up on life. It was a little stiff in the beginning, but we got back into our groove pretty quick. He met some other dude who sounded better than stupid fucking Robbie, but that's like saying a paper cut is better than having your arm amputated. He had some South Pacific Asian type name that I can't remember, but dude was stupid hot. I think the first time we met him Lilypad actually gasped.

It was a random weekday night when we went over there. Hot Asian had moved in with Damien already, which I thought was a little weird since they couldn't have been dating that long. But again, anything was an improvement over fucking Robbie so I didn't press it. The night wasn't that eventful. Hot Asian seemed like one of those overly attractive guys with the personality of a dumbbell. He looked like he was posing for a camera the whole time and didn't talk that much, but when he did it was always some story about getting wasted at the WeHo bars and how all the guys were hitting on him. He seemed pretty inconsequential, both to me and Damien, because once Damien bought the house he kicked Hot Asian to the curb.

Damien also made this new friend, Jacob, this twerpy guy who was completely in love with him. He'd never admit it but it was so obvious. He's one of those guys you know was the class nerd in school, the one on the sidelines at every dance who watched enviously as all the other kids had the best time while he was always alone and never got over it.

Every time Loverboy called Damien to hang out, it sounded like a date. He never suggested they go out with other people, and I don't actually know if he had any other friends. He was so possessive, it was weird. Damien told me they went to Fubar one time, which of course they did. Its name is an acronym for Fucked Up Beyond All Recognition, so that should tell you all you need to know. It's the appropriately dark trashy hookup bar at the opposite end of the strip from the rest of the gay clubs. It looks like a New York bar, really narrow with exposed brick all along the right wall, so at first glance it's totally my kind of divey joint. But the one time I went with Damien to investigate when we first started living together, I was immediately assaulted with hardcore dude porn on the TVs and a gogo "dancer" stroking his junk through a very tiny G-string on the platform next to the DJ booth. It was clear this establishment was not meant for me. These supposed "dancers" never seemed to actually dance when I saw them; they'd either stroke their penises or just thrust their pelvises so their junk flapped in everyone's face. I guess gay dudes like that? Well, their most popular night is the Thursday party Big Fat Dick, where guys take pics of their junk and hang them around the bar for everyone to vote for the best one at the end of the night. So yeah, I guess they like that.

So Loverboy and Damien go to Fubar at some point—I don't remember exactly when this story happened—and are dancing by the DJ booth. Some anonymous guy walks by that Damien thought was hot, which of course causes Damien to look him up and down. Out of nowhere, Loverboy slaps him across the face. Hard.

"What the fuck?"

"You were checking him out."

"And?"

"I'm standing right here."

In his anger, Damien slapped Loverboy across the face too, probably much harder than he was hit. He doesn't take well to being reprimanded in any way, especially not physically.

"We're not together, and even if in some alternate universe we were, you don't ever touch me like that."

Damien was pissed after that night, but Loverboy gave him some sob story apology about being so drunk and he didn't even remember what he said but he was sorry. Damien admitted they were both pretty drunk, and I think he secretly liked all the attention Loverboy gave him so they still hung out all the time. I didn't think anything of it when Damien told me, but with all of this and then what happened the week leading up to the...you know, it's hard not to be suspicious.

It was just a few days before...you know. The Tuesday or Wednesday before or something. Lilypad had heard this new restaurant called Conservatory was supposed to be good so we gave it a try. I don't like going out in boys' town anymore—not that I ever really liked it that much—but I figured how bad could it be? To be honest, the food was really good so that was a pleasant surprise.

But we got there and first thing I see is Damien sitting at this tiny two-person table with Loverboy. It looked weirdly intimate, which is never Damien's bag. I decided to walk over to check on him.

"Fancy meeting you here."

Damien looked up at me and I could instantly see his face change. Like he was looking for a save.

"Oh hey B."

"Thanks for the invite."

He laughed. "Yeah we just came down here to grab dinner real quick." He darted his eyes quickly toward Loverboy.

Damien had moved into this cool house up in Laurel Canyon not long before. He had this crazy boss Eileen who basically assaulted him and the company gave him a big settlement. He invited us over once after he moved in but that was really it; he'd become pretty much a hermit. Not that I could blame him—if I lived there I probably wouldn't leave too often either.

The house itself is great, really quaint and cute and all those lovable adjectives people use to describe newly remodeled homes. But the drive up there is such a pain in the ass, I don't think I could do that on the daily. The canyon roads are winding and narrow with a ton of blind curves, and almost everyone using them drives like they're petrified. I swear they're going a maximum of five miles an hour and it's infuriating. If you don't know how to drive on those roads, get the fuck off! Take a different route. It kills me. Lilypad always gets mad at me for driving too fast, but I got shit to do. I don't need to take a joy ride in my car to see the sights. Get to where you're going. The drivers in this city are the worst, and also super douchey recently. I've noticed a rise in the most ridiculous vanity license plates, which vanity license plates are high on the douche scale to begin with. I saw one that was just TVPRODCR on what I'm pretty sure was a used BMW from about 2012. Safe to say that guy's gonna be a registered sex offender in the near future.

But for Damien, it was rare for him to make the trek down the hill once he was home already, hence my surprise.

"You came all the way down just to grab dinner?"

"I came straight from work."

"Aw, who's feeding Stanley then?"

"He'll be fine."

"Hope he doesn't shit on your couch."

We both laughed. Stanley'd moved from shitting on Damien's bed to shitting on his couch when he got pissed, and being fed late was his number one reason for getting pissed.

"He's fine, thanks for the concern."

Lilypad was hungry and I could see her inching toward our table.

"Ok well have fun." I shot him my wide-eyed "signal if you need my help" look so he knew I'd be there if he needed me. He nodded and smiled.

I watched them on and off from across the restaurant the rest of the night and it all seemed mostly fine. Loverboy was a little touchy, which made me cringe cause I knew Damien wasn't enjoying it. Every time he laughed, he'd reach over to graze Damien across the table, as if that physical contact somehow emphasized how funny whatever he laughed at was. They drank a lot of wine so maybe he was just drunk, but either way he was annoying Damien.

We left before they did, and Damien was definitely drunk by then. I tried to give him a subtle sign as we headed out but Loverboy was too possessive of his attention and I didn't want to be obvious. We walked back to our place and I stopped outside the gate as Lilypad pulled the house keys from her bag.

"I think I'm gonna go check on Damien."

"Why? He looked fine."

"I just have a weird feeling."

Lilypad stared at me for a second. She didn't say anything to talk me out of it, but it felt like the words of protest were ready to march out of her mouth. She must've decided the fight wasn't worth it, because she leaned in and kissed me goodbye. As she opened the wrought iron gate, I walked back to the restaurant. When I rounded the corner on to Santa Monica Damien and Loverboy were right in front of me.

"What the fuck?" They startled me and that's usually my kneejerk reaction.

"Oh hey again." Loverboy was giggling about something so I don't even know if he registered that I was there.

"What're you guys doing?"

"Jacob and I just had dinner."

I laughed. He always stated the obvious when he was drunk. "I know that, I'm not an idiot. What're you doing now?"

He stepped toward me with a hazy grin on his face. "You love me."

When Damien gets that drunk, it's usually a quick downward spiral to vomitsville, and I really didn't want him to puke down my shirt again so I stepped back. "I do love you, but not when you treat me like a barf bag."

"You're my favorite."

He kept trying to paw at my shoulders to bring me closer, but in his drunken stupor he was more leaning on me. I had to swat him away before he knocked us both down, which he almost did and the surprise made me giggle. "Fuck off."

"You're the one who left me for your stupid girlfriend."

Damien's tone swiftly turned aggressive, which isn't that unusual when he's consumed that much alcohol. He stumbled in place a little, while Loverboy seemed to be overly interested in the garbage can on the corner. He picked at it like he was studying some ancient alien artifact.

I knew I had to tread carefully with Damien, otherwise this could turn ugly real fast. I softened my voice and reached my hands out, doing my best Mother-Teresa-helps-an-invalid pose.

"Damien, I didn't leave you. I tried to fix it—"

He swatted my hands away. "There's nothing to fix."

Drunk and obstinate Damien is not one you can contend with. I knew at this point he just needed to get home, and if I tried to push him anymore it would just keep getting worse.

"Okay I'm going to go home. You should go home too."

He stumbled back again but kept his balance, so I started walking away. When I looked back, he was already gone.

We didn't talk after that, and I feel really shitty that was my last conversation with him. I don't know what I would've done differently, because I never would've thought that'd be the last time I saw him. I don't know what happened with Loverboy that night, or the nights after, but it probably wasn't anything Damien wanted.

Then, on the Sunday after, the cops called me. Honestly I can't even remember what they said now. I was sitting on one of the stools at our kitchen counter eating a bowl of Honey Bunches of Oats (laugh if you must), and Lilypad handed me my phone cause an unknown number was calling me. Like any normal person I never answer an unknown call, but for some reason this time I did. I don't know why. I didn't feel compelled or anything, I just answered it, like I was meant to. And they told me what happened, and I just couldn't compute. It didn't make sense.

When I hung up, I told Lilypad and she ran over to hug me. I didn't hug back, not for any reason. I was just frozen. I couldn't cry right away because it just didn't make any sense. I actually called Damien to see if it was a joke, but obviously he didn't answer. When his voicemail came on and I heard his voice, that's when I collapsed and started sobbing.

Honestly, I still just can't believe it. I can't believe that he's gone. I'm still waiting for him to show up and be like, "Really? That's how I die?" He would've been pissed. I guess that sounds stupid, anyone would be pissed that they died. But Damien, if you see this, or feel it, or whatever from wherever you are...I'm sorry. I miss you. And I love you.

THE EX-BOYFRIEND

I met Damien at Motherlode. I was a bar back. They used to call me bare back. All the other guys who worked there were old and pervy. But I don't care I'm used to it. They thought I was hot. Older guys are into me. One time I had sex with this guy at the gym who was like fifty or something. I don't know he had gray hair but he was ripped so it was hot. He was going to the steam room and saw me changing and stopped and stared. His dick was already hard under his towel so I knew. Can I say dick is that ok? Or should I say penis? I went in there after him and he was sitting with his towel off and his penis was hard. I sat on it and he grabbed my butt and we had sex till we both came. It was hot. But I was working that night I met Damien and he came in for a drink. He was by himself. He sat at the bar and checked me out. I played like I didn't see him but I knew. Guys always think they're slick but I can tell. I was refilling the ice and he was like do you think this drink is like blah blah I don't know what he said. Who talks like that? And who doesn't know what they're drinking? I just laughed. He must've made a joke cause he liked that I laughed. He drank till I was done. I could tell he wanted to take me home. He was kind of hot so I was like ok. He's not really muscular like I usually like. He's kind of skinny fat but has a cute face so it's ok. I took a shot of tequila behind the bar and he came and grabbed my butt. I told him he wasn't allowed back there. He was like I don't follow rules. That made him so much hotter. I kissed him and we made out for a while. It was so hot. I could feel him getting hard and I was too. He was like let's get out of here. He took me back to his place and we had sex all night. It was the best sex. I blew him then he ate me out and we did it doggy style. I flipped over and he did it on top of me. Like face to face you know. Missionary or whatever. He called me Good Boy then pounded me till he came. I passed out and woke up on the couch. I don't remember getting there but his bitch of a roommate woke me up. Sorry but she is. She slammed the door and it scared the crap out of me. I was so tired I just went back to sleep. She's such a bitch. Her name is just B like the letter. Who does that? Who has just a letter for a name? Whatever she's a bitch. I woke up again when Damien was cooking in the kitchen. He made eggs and I almost stepped on his cat. He was like that's Stanley Kowalski watch out he bites. I couldn't get that stupid name for the longest time. Damien said I had to call him by his full name. Who does that? What cat has a full name? Stanley Kowalski was weird too. He always just sat and stared like he was going to kill me or something. But whatever he was nice to me. I mean he left me alone so I guess that's nice for him haha. He didn't try to scratch my eyes out. He never did anything he just stared and that was really weird. He was creepy I didn't like him. Damien made me eggs and they were really good. He made eggs a lot when we were dating. I can't cook so he never let me. When B woke up again she was still a bitch. We were on the couch watching tv and she came in and was like oh you're still here. I was like hi nice to meet you too. And she just walked into the kitchen. Bitch. She never liked me but I don't care. She doesn't like anyone probably. She doesn't have any friends you know. Like really none. The only person she ever hung out with other than Damien was her girlfriend. I can't believe she had a girlfriend. Who'd want to date someone that mean? There's a lot of people like her in LA. They're really mean for no reason. Like there's this guy I see at Gelson's all the time who always yells at me to get out of the way and calls me stupid. I'm like I'm not in your way go around and you don't even know me. How do you even know I'm stupid? A lot of people call me stupid. They're all mean. I know I'm not the smartest but I'm not stupid. I know some things. Everyone's got things they're good at and things they're not. Damien's not good at a lot of things. He's not good at changing tires but I am. My car used to break down all the time so I got really good at changing the tires. I mean it still breaks down a lot haha so I'm still good at it. But Damien never was. And B's not good at being nice. Like at all. So everyone's got something. And people always yell at me when I'm driving. Everyone in LA is an angry driver that's why I hate driving. And cause my car breaks down a lot. This one time I saw these two guys stop their cars on the freeway and they got into a full on fight. Like punches and everything. It was so crazy. I think it was the 405. I hate taking the freeway. I hate driving that's why I live in West Hollywood. I can walk everywhere. I got horny again on the couch and started grabbing Damien and he got hard right away. We went into his room and had sex again and I was extra loud so B would hear. She wasn't around when I left. She probably got mad or something. I didn't give Damien my number but I knew I'd see him again. Guys always want to see me again after they have sex with me. The next time we went out was a couple nights later I think. I thought he'd just come to Motherlode again but he didn't. He came by my place when I wasn't home and left a post it on the front door of my building that was like hi Robbie it's Damien call me. It was kind of weird but kind of cute. Who does that? Who even has post its? I don't know how he knew where I lived but whatever. It was good sex so I wanted to see him again. I called him and he was like let's have dinner. He wanted to go on a date not just have sex. He liked me. We went to a restaurant but I don't remember which one. Maybe that one by the Abbey I think. Yeah Sur. That's where we went. He didn't order a crazy drink again. I think he just had a vodka soda or something. I only drink tequila shots. But not like a ton of them. I'm not an alcoholic. Just one or two. Mixers have too many calories. We went back to his place and had sex again. He was really into me. B wasn't there this time. Stanley Kowalski sat on the dresser the whole time. It was weird. He just watched us having sex. Who does that? I asked Damien to kick him out but he was like he's fine. That made it weirder. Like why are you ok with Stanley Kowalski watching us have sex? But whatever the sex was good. He had me on my side which isn't my favorite. But then he flipped me on my stomach and that was good. I didn't stay over that night. He had a big interview or something the next day. He called me like a week later. I gave him my number this time. I always let the guy call me. Never call him that way they don't think you're desperate. He asked me if I wanted to come over that night. He was really horny I could tell. I went over and we had sex like three times. He threw me on the couch right when I got there and ripped my clothes off. He blew me and I pushed him back and rode him till we both came. He got a beer but he didn't have tequila so I didn't drink anything. Beer has too many calories and makes my stomach hurt. I mean it makes me fart. Haha I can't believe I said that. We watched tv a little. He said he got the job he interviewed for so I was like that's cool. B wasn't there. She was at her girlfriend's. He started talking about the movie we were watching but I didn't know it. Michelle Sarah or something was in it and she went to Harvard or something. I remember she told someone to suck her dick. Sorry to say dick that was the line she didn't say penis. But it was funny. He was like in love with her. He had a movie poster for I Know What You Did Last Summer in his room. She was in it and her face was huge on the poster. I never saw it I don't like those movies. Damien loved movies. Like a lot. He wanted to be a producer or actor or writer or something. Probably whatever he could do as long as it was movies. That's why he moved out here. He told me this idea he had for a movie where this kid and his best friend were attacked in their high school by these crazy monsters but you never saw them. It was a scary movie cause those were his favorite. I don't like those kind of movies but it sounded cool. Maybe he could have been a writer but I don't think an actor. He's cute but not actor cute. Maybe he could play the nerdy friend or something. But he's not like Channing Tatum hot. He was so good in that stripper movie. I wish I went to that strip club haha. All those guys were so hot. But after we finished the movie he took me to his room and we had sex again. Doggy style cause he loved my ass oops sorry butt. All guys like my butt and he really did. He said he couldn't get enough. I was tired so I fell asleep. This time he didn't move me cause I woke up in bed. It was the middle of the night. I had to pee so went to the bathroom. It was like two or three and a light was on in the living room. I went to see and some girl was sleeping on the couch. I thought she'd wake up if she heard me so I coughed but she didn't. So I went and peed and went back to bed. I thought about waking Damien up to have sex again but I was tired so just went back to sleep. When I woke up he was already up. I could hear him talking outside and figured it was B. I listened for a second but couldn't hear what they were saying. She was freaking out about something. Like she was mad at someone but she always was. I didn't want to see her but I was bored in his room so I had to get up. I went out and she was like oh you're still around? And I was like yeah. She's such a bitch. But the girl on the couch wasn't there. Turns out it was her girlfriend and she just left. That's why B was so mad. I'd leave too if I were stuck with B. Damien was like it was great seeing you. So I was like yeah I got to go. And I left. And B made some stupid comment like miss you or something. But Damien kissed me goodbye. He liked me. He grabbed my butt again too. We started hanging out more not just having sex. We went on a hike in Runyon Canyon that weekend. He got mad cause everyone kept checking me out. He was like why does everyone keep staring at us? I was like cause they're checking me out. He was jealous. I like when guys get jealous. That's how you know they like you. We went back to his place and had sex after. We were all sweaty so it was hot. He bent me over the side of the bed and we did it standing up. I didn't stay over again. He said he had something. But he text me a couple times later about hanging out but had to cancel every time. He started his job and said it was a lot. His boss was really mean he kept saying what bitch she was. She always yelled at him and I think threw things at him once. I don't know I think that's what he said but I don't remember. People can be really mean so I believe it. He wanted to see me but couldn't. I got it. My work can be a lot too. But on the weekend he told me he had to see me. I tried to get him to come to my apartment but he said it was easier for me to go there. He said it was cause of my roommates. But he had a roommate too so I didn't get it. And at least my roommates are nice. Well kind of. They can be mean too but mostly they're nice. They just like to party. Like this one time my roommate Jack had a big birthday party and invited all these guys over and everyone ended up having sex with each other. I picked this hot guy who was like a hairstylist or colorist or something. I don't think he knew Jack though. I don't know how he got there. But he was super hot. He ripped my underwear off he was so excited to have sex with me. Like really ripped them off. It was so hot. But they were a new pair I just got from Chi Chi La Rue's. I wish he hadn't ripped them in half. They were expensive. But it's ok it was hot. And it was before I even met Damien so it was ok. I'm not a cheater. He kept saying I had to come over I had to come over. He really wanted me. I didn't want to see B but whatever. When I got there he pulled me right into his room. He pounded me really hard that time. He said after that his boss was a total bitch to him. She screamed and called him bad names. I was like that sucks. He told some crazy stories about her but I don't remember. She sounded psycho. He was getting her fired cause she was so psycho. I didn't know you could fire someone for being psycho but he said he was. He always said come on Eileen when he talked about her cause her name was Eileen. I think that was one of his movie quotes or something. I don't know I didn't get it. He always said movie quotes but I never knew what they were. Anytime I didn't know what he was saying I just laughed cause I figured it was some movie quote. He liked that. I was thirsty so I went out to get some water. Right when I left the kitchen B came in. She was with her girlfriend the girl from the couch. I can never remember her name so I always call her the girl from the couch haha. She was like you could put some clothes on. B said that not the girl from the couch. She said it really mean. B's such a bitch. I didn't get dressed cause we were alone. It's not my fault she came home. I didn't know. I went back into Damien's room to get dressed and he went to talk to B. She was yelling cause she was pissed about me. She said nasty things but I don't remember. She's such a bitch. When I got dressed the girl from the couch was in the hall outside B's room. She just stood there watching them fight. She looked a lot better than before. Probably cause she wasn't sleeping on a couch haha. Her shoes were really cool too. I don't know why I always notice people's shoes. I guess I like them a lot. Damien's shoes were kinda boring. He just had sneakers and stuff. And not cool sneakers just like dad sneakers. B's were pretty cool. I wanted most of the shoes she wore. And her girlfriend's were like patent leather high top Converse or something. They were really cool. I was gonna say something but Damien came over. He was like you should probably go. He walked me out and kissed me goodbye again. We would've hung out more if B wasn't such a bitch. He always talked about her like she told him what to do. He was always like B said I should do this and B doesn't like that so I can't do it. I don't know why he always listened to her. It was like whatever she said he did. And I don't know what her problem is. A lot of people are like that in LA. They just make up problems. Maybe they're bored or something. Or maybe they're just mean. I don't know. B's probably just mean cause she has no friends. But maybe if she weren't so mean she'd have friends. I never really saw her again after that night. She was never around when I was over so that was good. And I don't know why he cared so much about what she thought. He picked me up one time to go to dinner at Marco's before we had sex and Break Free by Ariana Grande came on. It's my favorite song I love dancing to it. So I was like I love this song. And he was like this song is the worst B hates it and changed the channel. She wasn't even in the car who cares? He was like she says Ariana Grande looks like a baby prostitute. Who says that? Babies can't be prostitutes that's gross. It was like that with everything. If B didn't like it Damien didn't like it. Like he never wanted to go to any other bars except in West Hollywood cause B said all the others were lame. That's so not true. MJ's was really fun they had this foam party that always got crazy. They had a little dance floor in the back corner that they'd fill with foam and you couldn't see anything and everyone just felt each other up. One time this really hot guy started making out with me and I jerked him off on the dance floor. He had a hot body at least I couldn't see his face. It was really hot but I think I swallowed some of the foam when we were making out which was gross. I got sick that night. I might've drank too much too cause I had like six tequila shots. But it could've been the foam too. It smelled a little it was gross. But the guy was hot and had a really nice dick. Oops sorry penis. And Faultline has a really fun beer bust every Sunday. I never drink beer cause it makes me feel fat and I like to keep my shirt off. And the farting haha. This one time I had to pee and this guy followed me into the bathroom. When I was at the urinal peeing he pulled my pants down and ate me out. It was really hot. He wasn't that cute but it was still fun. But Damien never wanted to go. He said B would kill him. We would've stayed together if it wasn't for her. We had a lot of fun together. Like this one time he took me to his fancy work party at this restaurant in Beverly Hills. It was called Bergeron I think like the guy who hosted America's Funniest Home Videos. It was the fanciest dinner I've ever been to. I don't even know what it cost. Probably like a thousand dollars or something. And we got dressed up in suits and ties. I could tell he thought I looked so hot in a suit. I look really good in suits. I mean

I only have one but I look really good in it. He kept looking me up and down and smiling. When we were walking up the stairs he grabbed my butt and leaned in to smell me and was like are you wearing cologne? And I was like yeah. I stole some of my roommate's CK One. I didn't say that to him but I did. He kind of grunted and grabbed my butt tighter. I knew he thought I looked hot. We got to the top of the stairs and gave his name. They knew exactly where to seat us. They pulled the chair out for me and everything. His boss was already there with a couple other people. I don't remember who. They all said who they were but I can't remember. I remember her though cause she was an even bigger bitch than he said. Right when we sat down she was like you're late. And Damien was like it's seven-thirty now isn't that when the reservation is? And she was just like you're late. She grilled me too and I just answered as quick as I could. She was scary. She was like where are you from what do you do who are you? Who does that? She was crazy. She made some mean comment about me being stupid or something but I didn't care. She didn't even know me. But Damien said something to her. Like you can't talk to him that way. He was protecting me. He liked to protect me. If we were waiting in line somewhere he'd stand behind me and wrap his arms over my shoulders. I like when guys do that that's why I like taller guys. He did that when we were getting cupcakes at Sprinkles at the Grove. He loved dessert. That's why he was skinny fat. We were waiting in line and he wrapped his arms around me and kissed my ear. It was nice. He liked me that's why he did it. He started wiggling his waist so his penis rubbed against my butt. And then he laughed and bit my ear. Not like a hard bite or anything. Like a nice bite. But he still wanted to wait for his cupcakes. He was just playing around cause he liked me. I liked when he played around like that. And the food at his work dinner was amazing too. They had this fried chicken and I know it sounds stupid but it was the best fried chicken I've ever had. Way better than KFC. I ate all of it and the mashed potatoes. I never eat anything on a date but this was so good. Damien was pissed after dinner cause his boss was such a bitch. He was mad that she was so mean to me. He wanted to take care of me. I like when guys take care of me. I hoped he wouldn't want to have sex cause I felt gross after eating all the fried chicken. But as soon as we got in the car he grabbed my leg and started rubbing it and I knew. Sometimes you just got to make it work. We didn't even make it back to his place. He parked the car on one of those side streets behind Pavilions and we had sex in the car. It was so quiet I was scared to make any noise. But that made it kind of hot. Like we might get caught. One of the streets over there is called Dicks haha. I think that's the one we had sex on cause we thought it was funny. He put his seat back first and I rode him in the driver's seat till I came. Then he wanted to do it doggy style so we put my seat down and he did it till he came. He didn't say it but I think I helped calm him down when he was angry. There was this other time he and B got in a big fight. He called me and was talking all fast like I can't believe her she's such a bitch she only thinks about herself and stuff. She like ditched him for her girlfriend or something. I'm trying to remember. Like they were supposed to go somewhere or see something and she bailed on him. I don't remember. But he was pissed. He asked me to come over and we had sex all over his apartment. Like seriously all over. We did it in the kitchen on the counter and on the table. We did it on the couch and the floor and standing at the window in the living room. We even went into her room and did it on her bed. I think it was when she was moving out cause now I remember there were all these boxes in her room. Yeah. He was mad cause she moved out with him and moved in with her girlfriend. I felt a little weird but he was like it'll be so hot. It was pretty hot. He got super into it. I did too. It kind of felt like we were going to get in trouble or something. But the next day was when he text me. It was so bad. I think B found out and freaked on him and he felt bad. Cause he was super into me. But I don't know why he'd blame me. He was the one who wanted to have sex in her room. But I don't know why else he'd break up with me. And he broke up with me over text. That's so shitty. Sorry but it was. Who does that? He was just like I don't think this is working and we should break up I'm sorry. Who says that? We just had sex all day yesterday and it's not working? It was working pretty good all day yesterday. And he didn't say I love you yet but I know he was going to. Like he'd always call me after a bad day. This one time he called me and was like about to start crying. His boss screamed at him in front of all his coworkers and B was always at her girlfriend's. He was like I don't have anyone and am really sad. I told him I could come over cause I was just finishing up at the gym but he said no. I felt bad for him and wanted to be there for him. I get sad like that sometimes too so I know what it's like. You just want someone to hug you. He was a good hugger too. After we had sex he'd always hug me and hold me. He was always warm but it was nice. Even when it was really hot outside it felt nice. But you only call the people you love like that. So why would he break up with me? I kind of flipped out after he text me and sent him like fifty texts in a row. It probably freaked him out so when I called him to talk he wouldn't answer the phone. So that made me flip out even more and that wasn't great. I drank a bunch of tequila shots at the bar that night so I was probably drunk. I remember going to his place but I don't remember what I said or what he said. It probably wasn't great. The next day I woke up and didn't feel great. Not just cause of the hangover. I felt bad that I let myself do that. I drove home to Riverside to help feel better. My mom always makes me chilaquiles when I'm down. She makes them the best they always make me feel better. I decided I wouldn't talk to him again unless he called me. He never did so I haven't talked to him since. Until the week before it happened when I ran into him at Gelson's. I was going in to get more protein powder and he was coming out with a box from the bakery. He was all surprised to see me and was like hey Robbie you look great. Cause I do. I've been going to the gym all the time so am pretty ripped. Every guy's been hitting on me. Like this super hot Indian guy at the gym. I was doing chest flies and I could see him staring at me from the squatting machine. He was so hot and totally wanted me. He looked Indian but after we hooked up he said he was Asian or something. I don't get it but whatever he was hot. I didn't go up to him but he followed me into the locker room and we had sex. He pushed me against my locker and made out with me then took me to the showers and pulled my shorts down and we had sex. It was so hot. Way better than Damien. So I was like thanks. To Damien. Well I said thanks to the Indian guy too but not really haha. I said it to Damien at Gelson's. I didn't say Damien looked great too cause he looked like he put on a few pounds. He was getting stuff from the bakery so probably eating a lot of dessert. And he was like we should get together again. Which I know means I really want to have sex with you again. I was like sure but I didn't really want to see him again. He had his chance and he messed it up. There are a ton of other guys who like me and want to have sex with me. Like I went to Big Fat Dick after I saw him and won and had sex with the promoter Mario in the back. That's the name of the party I didn't swear. He's a hot zaddy bear with all these tattoos and a moustache. He kind of looks like Mario from Super Mario Brothers. But a hot Mario. He was eyeing me all night I could tell. I had a couple tequilas so I entered the contest and won. Once he saw the pic of my dick I knew. Oops that time I did swear sorry. Once he saw the pic of my penis I knew. All guys love my penis so that's why I won. When everyone cheered the most for my pic I went up and could tell he wanted me. He grabbed my butt and kind of grunted in my ear so I knew. We went in the back and he blew me and then turned me around and we had sex on some boxes of alcohol. The cheap ones not like Absolut or anything. The plastic bottles that won't break. I would've been so nervous to break all those bottles haha. It was so hot. But after Damien walked away with his desserts I never saw him again. Honest. I ran into B and her girlfriend on that Thursday or Friday or something. She's still a bitch. I was walking home from the gym and saw them. She was like oh it's you. I didn't even say hi I don't care. And she was like weren't you crying in the street the last time I saw you? And I was like yeah last time I saw you I was fucking Damien all over your bed. Sorry but that's what I really said. And she deserved it. She got so mad. She didn't even say anything but I could tell she was so pissed. She wanted to kill me. I didn't care I just walked away. And then I heard about this. It sucks. But maybe if Damien had been nicer he wouldn't have ended up like this. And sorry I swore so much.

THE BEST FRIEND'S GIRLFRIEND

yeah. it was weird. it's always strange meeting your girlfriend's friends but damien was especially so. they went beyond codependent. it was like, an obsessive need or compulsion toward each other.

of course i didn't realize this when i met b. actually i met damien before i even met her. it wasn't the greatest intro for me so i've never brought it up to her, and she hasn't either so i don't think she knows. it's probably for the best tbh, i don't know what i'd say to her if it did come up. "oh hey i just realized your best friend is the random guy who borderline harassed me completely unprovoked in a public setting?" not really a great ice breaker on a first date imo.

it started w/ my friend alberta roping our group into a trip downtown. she's a huge jim henson fan, she's been trying to get a job at their studio on la brea since forever. so of course the second cinespia announced they were screening *Labyrinth* the weekend before halloween she sent invites to everyone. and since we all love an excuse to dress up we each got our tickets the day they went on sale.

we met at my friend ricky's house to get ready together. i was supposed to go as sarah from the masquerade fantasy sequence, and it would've been amazing if it'd actually worked. the gown i ordered was perfect and i got all these extensions and hair accessories so i would've nailed it. but despite my internet stalking the stupid website who made the gown, they didn't ship in time so my great idea was ruined. of course by that point it was too late to find anything that would work for the masquerade, and pivoting to a new look at that late of an hour would've been too much stress for me. i love a costume but a last minute scramble all over town is way too much anxiety for me. so i decided not to dress up. plus i don't do well w/ disappointment so i was kicking my feet in the dirt a little tbh.

when i got to ricky's alberta was already getting her feathers on. she went even more over the top than i did, she was going as one of the fireys and hand dyed all these feathers that she glued on to various sleeves, shirts and wings. she never messes around w/ a costume, especially not one that revolves around jim henson.

ricky was just hanging out {he was going as the inchworm and found a site that sold worm costumes, so random}, so he just had to get into it right before we left.

mike and patti weren't there yet of course, they were perpetually on their own time. but they said their bowie and hoggle wouldn't take long.

ricky, being the control freak that he is, insisted that i dress up as something so went to his costume box to get me some generic 80s garb. it was super lame but i was too annoyed about my original costume to argue. apparently ricky didn't agree w/ my no-costume-is-better-than-a-shitty-one theory.

he found a blazer w/ huge shoulder pads, a not-quite-matching long pleated skirt and started teasing my hair out. they weren't even cool thrift store finds, they looked like something out of a cheesy jc penney catalogue he stole from his mom as a kid. my halloween costumes of yore were cringing w/ regret. and i never realized it but he and i are v similar in size. everything he had fit me pretty perfectly. we just had to safety pin the back of the skirt so it was a little tighter, but that was it. i wish we had more similar personal styles but b is more in line w/ what he wears, at least in his everyday wardrobe. and they are definitely not the same size.

by the time we'd finished picking out my patchwork look mike and patti still weren't there. ricky isn't one to be late so he text stalked them until they finally showed up. everyone was pretty aggro w/ each other, except alberta who was in her own little jim henson bliss.

when we finally arrived downtown {after mike and patti's quick changes} the theater of course was packed. movie nerds have a knack for punctuality, and the fans of *Labyrinth* put them to shame. we basically had to shove our way in, and in another moment of great annoyance everyone wanted to go somewhere different. mike wanted a drink, alberta had to pee, ricky just wanted to get to our seats and patti kept talking to the wrong ppl b/c she couldn't see through her hoggle mask. i just wanted everyone to stop bumping into me. i'm normally a pretty patient person, but crowded places w/ ppl shoving each other to move every step of the way aren't my fave, and that night especially i really couldn't be bothered. i probably should've stayed home.

miraculously we found some seats in the mezzanine. ricky couldn't figure out how to sit in his costume and if i'd been in a better mood i'm sure it would've been hilarious. i think alberta drank a dozen shots of espresso or something b/c she couldn't sit still. i was trying to will the movie to be over so i could go home but it hadn't even begun. it was one of those nights when everything my friends did made me want to curse them out. i love my friends but sometimes they can be so obnoxious.

the movie finally started and i thought i'd finally get some peace. about halfway through, maybe less, out of nowhere some guy walks up next to me and whispers, "if you ever come between us i will end you."

i looked up at him from the corner of my eye. of course now i know it was damien, but at the time he was just some rando w/ bad impressionist bowie makeup. it looked like he let a three-year-old put it on. and he had the cheapest plastic wig that i guess was meant to be similar to bowie's from the movie {mike's was much better} and his eyes were dark w/ fury.

we'd never seen each other before but he looked at me like i'd killed his puppy. i had no idea what he was talking about but he clearly meant it. he lingered for a minute, maybe to see if i'd respond? but i had no idea what to say, nor really cared to figure out what was happening anyway, so i just stared at the screen. after a minute he just walked away.

ricky leaned over to me and asked, "do you know that guy?"

"nope, never seen him before."

"i think he thought i was a child. he told me how cute i was and patted me on the head." again i didn't know how to respond so i just grunted.

ricky took my non-verbal response as an invitation to continue. "what'd he say to you?"

"nothing that made any sense."

by that point i was over everyone and everything and just really wanted it all to end. i decided to ignore everyone from that point on and laser focus on the movie. i have a pretty good talent for tuning out the world when i want. sarah's adventures were the only thing going on for me in that moment, nothing was going to divert my attention. when the movie finished i made a quick irish exit and hurried straight to the safety of my apartment.

when i randomly met b at a coffee bean i was in a much better mood. for starters i hadn't missed out on one of my best costumes to date. and not twenty minutes prior i aced my renaissance art midterm so i was feeling pretty good about myself.

there was no line at coffee bean that day {i like to think the universe was smiling w/ me} so i walked right up and ordered my regular. when he asked for my name i told the barista what i always tell them, "lily, like lily pad."

it started when alberta and i ordered dinner one night years ago. the guy at chin chin couldn't understand me and that's the only thing i could think of. alberta was laughing hysterically when i got off the phone and said now she could only see me like Kermit the Frog. that made me laugh too so i've said it ever since.

it also led to the greatest costume i ever actually wore—that halloween i was a lily pad to alberta's Kermit the Frog. the highlight? when i laid down on santa monica blvd and she sat on me to sing "the rainbow connection". we got on ktla w/ that one.

anyway. b started chatting me up while we waited for our coffees. she's a total sexy nerd, my type to the v last details. she had on these awesome vintage glasses {they turned out to be warby parkers, but they looked super vintage} and these fitted flooded trousers that hugged her ass and thighs perfectly. she was so beautiful.

i could tell she was flirting b/c, you know, you can always kinda tell. she walked me to the parking lot and teasingly asked if i was going to ask her out. and i figured why not? so i did. and yes, i know—lesbians jumping right into everything. but why wait? i didn't have plans that night, she clearly didn't either so why shouldn't we go out? not that i need anyone's validation, but it's not that ridiculous.

so i picked her up at her place. she lived in the cutest little apartment, i was really jealous of it tbh. it was probably a single family home at some point, and whoever owns it divided it into two apartments. hers was in the back of the house so you had to walk up the driveway to the entrance, which was on the side of the house. it was this cobblestone driveway, bungalow-style house—everything right out of my dreams.

i was feeling really good when i knocked on the door. she opened right away and looked even more like my dreams. she had on this perfectly fitted plaid shirt that made her breasts look like heaven. i think whoever made it specifically designed it to highlight her boobs, and job well done. and those same perfect trousers that hugged her legs. it was really all i could do not to grab her ass.

i could tell she was a little nervous. b's never good at hiding her feelings, especially when she has any kind of nerves. she just said hi, so i smiled and complimented her to try to make her comfortable.

then, out of nowhere, i hear from behind her, "she's been dancing around like that for thirty minutes."

i knew that voice before i even saw him. i'd know it if i were blindfolded in a sensory deprivation room. she stepped out of the way and there he was, sitting on the couch.

"sorry that's my roommate damien."

of course he was her roommate. it felt like a verse from alanis morissette's song "ironic". it's pretty close actually, we're just the queer version of it. "it's like meeting the girl of my dreams, then meeting her psycho roommate."

i guess i don't mean totally psycho, i don't like casual judgments and stereotypes of serious mental disorders, but there's definitely something off about him. he's perfectly nice to your face but if you go even a millimeter deeper you'll find some devious intention. but then that describes a lot of ppl in la tbh.

thankfully b didn't want to hang out there either so we took off pretty quick. as we walked down the driveway toward the street i felt compelled to reiterate how amazing she looked and highlight how perfect the shirt jacket was.

"you really do look amazing. that shirt is perfect on you."

"oh thanks. damien picked it out for me."

in the moment that comment was only a little weird to me, but as we dated i realized just how ingrained his opinion is in almost everything she does. she doesn't own a single piece of clothing that he hasn't at least had approval over, if not explicitly chosen.

and it extends beyond her wardrobe. he has influence over the movies she likes, the music she listens to, even what restaurants to eat at.

for one of our dates i wanted to do something a little out of the box so i suggested we grab tacos from ricky's fish tacos, this amazing food truck i discovered. she audibly gasped when i said the words "food truck".

"oh no, damien says you can never trust a food truck. they're mobile disease centers."

he'd never even eaten at a food truck, let alone this specific one. i've been there multiple times along w/ many other ppl, and everyone raves about it.

and w/ movies, forget about it. i learned v quickly not to make any recommendations. there's not a single movie title that she wouldn't come back w/ "damien heard it's so heinous" or "damien said it's literally unwatchable" or something like that. it was like he was her conscious.

also i have no idea what movies he actually likes since apparently every one i've considered watching is terrible. in his mind if sarah michelle gellar doesn't star in it the movie's not worth his precious time. i can't even get into his obsession w/ her, it defies all logic.

after a while i understood her valuation of his opinion to a certain extent. she had so many insecurities around her self-image when they met and he was the first person to really help her through those.

i didn't realize how delicate she still was until our 4th or 5th date. i suggested we try the tasting kitchen out in venice, it has a really solid menu and one time i ate at their communal table next to emma watson. normally i'm not impressed by celebrity but my inner Harry Potter nerd was ecstatic to be so close to Hermione.

i think b appreciated the change in scenery too since damien always wanted to stay in the three block radius that encapsulates weho. i don't know why gay guys are such nesters. lesbians always take the rap for that but the gays are really the ones who always go to the same places to hang around the same ppl. wow that's super generalizing, sorry. i'm sure that's not true of every gay man, but it definitely applies to all the ones i've ever met.

anyway, b and i go to the tasting kitchen and it's super romantic. they have the perfect low lighting so it feels intimate but not so dark that you can't see the person you're w/.

they sat us at one of the communal tables so we sat close, angled toward each other w/ her right leg on the footrest of my chair between my legs. we laughed looking through the menu together b/c she didn't know what half the ingredients were—it's one of those restaurants that prides itself on using atypical products. black futsu pumpkin? pea pistou? super pretentious but the food is v good so i give them a pass. tbh i think they just make up words to see if anyone's actually reading.

it was all going really well until the waiter showed up.

"hello miss." he addressed me first, then turned to b. "good evening sir."

b's whole demeanor immediately changed. her grand smile wiped off her face and she shrunk back in her seat. i could tell she didn't know what to say or do.

"excuse you, this is my girlfriend."

i can be a little reactive when i feel protective of someone i'm close w/, so the words blurted out of my mouth. the waiter instantly got as uncomfortable as b.

"i'm so sorry."

b tried to wave it off. "it's fine."

after my reactiveness i get obstinate in situations like these, so i don't let things go. and i was not about to here.

"it's not fine. maybe you shouldn't be so presumptuous and place so much importance on other ppl's gender. maybe you should be more concerned w/ respecting individuals as human beings."

of course he was dumbfounded, which i have to admit i enjoyed a little.

"i'm really sorry. first round's on me."

his response was appropriate and genuine so i didn't feel the need to press on.

"thank you. we haven't decided on anything yet, so give us a minute."

"of course."

he shuffled off quickly in his embarrassment. he was a blonde hair blue eyed straight cis man {an assumption i feel v supported in making} who i'm sure was from some midwest state not far from where i grew up. he'd probably never seen a couple like us before, which doesn't excuse his behavior but at least explains it.

when i looked back at b she was staring straight into my eyes w/ a smile. it startled me tbh.

"what?"

"you called me your girlfriend."

i didn't realize i'd said it, and it wasn't a conscious decision. describing our dating status would've been lengthy and the waiter probably would've assumed that i was on a date w/ a man. calling her my girlfriend was the gender specificity he needed to realize his mistake, but i hadn't thought about the statement it made about our relationship.

"sorry, it just came out—"

she leaned in and kissed me, her hands gently grasping either side of my face. it was somewhere between a peck and a full-fledged make out. not too much to be embarrassed to do in public, but not a quick sneak so no one notices. and b is an amazing kisser. luscious is the word that comes to mind to describe her lips.

she pulled back and her smile returned. "i liked it."

"me too," was all i could put together after that beautiful kiss.

so needless to say our relationship took off pretty well. she wanted to spend a lot of time at her place unfortunately, which meant i had to be creative about convincing her not to. at first it worked pretty well, but i couldn't avoid being around damien completely. he never acknowledged coming up to me at *Labyrinth* and i def wasn't going to mention it. what would i say to him—"hey why'd you come up to me randomly and threaten my life?"

plus i'm sure he would've made it into some kind of episode w/ b and he's always a sensitive topic for her, even more than her parents. i can tell her that her parents suck and she would likely agree, but if i suggest that damien might not be nice she wants us to go to therapy. and by us i mean the three of us—her, damien and me.

one of the first times we hung out w/ damien was the most uncomfortable night of my life. b had been begging me to have dinner at her place so i could get to know him. it was v important to her that we were friends and she was not quiet about it.

i dodged it for a few weeks w/out notice but after the 5th "oh yeah that sounds good, but what if we went to fill-in-the-blank restaurant for dinner instead?" she clearly wasn't going to let me out of it.

the interrogation began over the phone, which worked in my favor since she couldn't see my face.

"are you trying to avoid hanging out w/ damien?"

i rolled my eyes but kept the pitch of my voice high to hide my disdain.

"of course not. i'm just in the mood to go out."

"do you have a problem w/ him? do you not like him?"

"i don't even know him. don't read into this."

"i really want you guys to get along, it's important to me."

the ship was sinking and i couldn't figure out a way to scoop the water out fast enough. i started pacing.

"i know."

"i need it to be important to you too."

"it is."

i let out a silent sigh. i couldn't argue more, so i was forced into dinner one night later that week.

i bought a bottle of wine after drinking half the one i was planning to bring. b said she was going to cook something that was meant to be a surprise, which i was looking forward to. i do love going out but a home cooked meal from the one you love is special, even more so when it's the first time.

it was also the first time we were going to spend the night together, which i could tell made her really excited. she's not much of a cook so i think that was her way of making it even more of an event. i was a little bummed that i had to share these first times w/ damien, but i couldn't voice that to b w/out some serious blowback.

when i got to her place it smelled like a rosemary chicken type situation. she opened the door and i kissed her as i walked in.

"it smells amazing. what're you making?"

her face sunk. "nothing anymore."

"what do you mean?"

"damien wants to order instead."

i was about to retort w/ a less than polite comment when damien walked out from his room. he forced a gentle smile.

"i'm in the mood for pad thai."

my stance grounded in retaliation.

"i'm allergic to peanuts."

b was surprised and i think a little upset that she didn't know this about me. "you are?"

"they'll have something you can eat, i'm sure."

he sat on the couch and stared right at me. he was such an antagonist in such a passive aggressive way. he could've just peed all around b to mark his territory instead.

"you don't mind do you?" he asked w/ a tone and a look that i knew meant he was begging for a challenge.

one of b's biggest faults is her severe avoidance of confrontation, so i chose to spare her and not play into his game.

"of course not, i'll be fine. like you said, i'm sure they'll have something i can eat."

b leaned in close to me. "if you go into anaphylactic shock i'll give you mouth to mouth."

she winked to make it cute, so even in my annoyance i gave her a pass. she ran into the kitchen to grab menus.

"you can sit down." he said it less as an invitation and more as giving me permission.

i sat in the leather ikea armchair w/ matching ottoman directly facing him.

"it's nice to see you again." w/out b in the room i didn't try to hide my tone as much.

"i'm sure it is."

b rushed back in shuffling through their kitchen stash. "so we've got sweet chili thai, kung pao bistro—not really thai but in the asian family. pa oord noodles, nathalee thai. stop me if anything sounds good."

damien smiled faux-graciously. "i'll let our guest of honor decide."

i matched his smile. "i'm fine w/ whatever."

"well sweet chili thai is my fave so i'm going w/ that."

b sat on the couch next to damien, threw the rest of the menus on the table and passed that one to me. we ordered and i found a salad that had no means of contact w/ any sort of peanut.

74

and then we sat around and waited.

out of nowhere damien started. "so you've never seen *Scream?*"

to center myself i took a beat. "what?"

"the movie *Scream.* you've never seen it?"

"no i saw it, a long time ago."

b scooted a little forward on the couch, noticeably uncomfortable. "i told damien i didn't think you'd seen it."

"are you a big fan?" damien remained perfectly unmoved.

of course i was not about to succumb to his intimidation tactics, so i matched his unmovedness. "not a big fan. i like it i guess."

"so why'd you quote it when you asked b out?"

i legit had no idea what he was talking about. i tried to figure out from b's face what to make of all this, but she just looked embarrassed.

"i didn't."

"he thinks you were quoting it when you said you still haven't told me your name and i asked why you wanna ask me out on a date."

"but you hadn't told me your name."

"those are the lines from the movie." he stared only at me through the whole conversation.

i smiled my perky smile, suddenly realizing that this win would soon be mine.

"i just made a statement. if she followed up w/ the next line then wouldn't that mean she quoted the movie?"

"no." he didn't like losing even more than i did, and right then he knew he had.

"whatever, it's just a funny thing he thought you did. damien loves scary movies."

b laughed to try to kill the tension. it half worked. maybe a quarter.

we made idle chit chat the rest of the time until the food came. tbh i didn't hear much b/c i kept trying to avoid damien's stare. he just watched me the entire time, that same stupid grin plastered on his face. he was clearly trying to unnerve me. i've never seen someone be so still for so long.

we ate in the living room while watching tv. damien put on some smg movie b/c that's all he could ever watch. she was a pop star who was sad or something? i don't know i wasn't really paying attention. forest whitaker was in it though and i kept wondering why. i really like him but he can def do better than whatever this was. also brendan fraser was in it and i was also like why? this was long before his brenaissance, so i was really more like why is brendan fraser in anything.

going into this night i was worried about trying to incorporate damien as a third into my budding relationship, but what i came to realize as the night progressed was that i was a third wheel to their relationship. even just from a physical location standpoint, i was on the outs in the chair while they shared the couch.

b would occasionally reach over to squeeze my forearm or thigh, but the majority of the night she spent turned toward damien laughing at or joining in on his commentary for the movie. which i have to say, from a purely objective observer, was not funny.

since damien hijacked our night and made it into whatever he wanted, i pretended to get tired before the movie finished. i'm not the best actor so i'm sure it was obvious, but what do i care. i yawned really loud and stretched obnoxiously.

b was cozied up into the couch and looked at me. "are you tired already?"

"yeah, it's weird. i think i'm ready for bed."

damien had his head on the back of the couch and feet on the coffee table, like he was laying down.

"you can go home if you want." jerk.

b turned to him softly. "she's staying here tonight."

"oh."

you've never seen someone shut down a conversation like damien.

i moved my hand on top of b's and squeezed it. thankfully she got the signal.

"i guess i'm a little tired too. shall we?"

damien's face couldn't hide his displeasure. i smiled knowing i'd won again.

"yeah i think so."

we both got up.

"nice to see you again damien." i made a point to say that as b walked me to her room.

"yeah. i hope the tv isn't too loud."

i shut the door before he could finish.

b went straight to her closet and rifled through. "i think i have some pjs you can borrow."

i was already undressed and laid across the bed. apparently she didn't see this coming b/c she giggled when she turned.

"what're you doing?"

"it's not terribly late, and we are still reasonably young." i patted the bed beside me.

she closed the closet door, her vixen smirk slowly revealing itself.

"i thought you were tired?"

"no, i said i was ready for bed."

she took her clothes off and crawled into bed toward me.

"ah sneaky."

she kissed me and i pulled her down. i'm pretty certain that damien had muted the tv and was listening to hear what we were doing. he's such a creeper, but let him hear what real love-making sounds like.

from then on i think b realized that damien and i weren't destined to be close. she tried occasionally but i got away w/ shutting it down for a while, but after a couple weeks she became persistent again.

we were having dinner at masa when she brought it up. it's this amazing little italian place in echo park that has the best deep dish pizza. and b's a chicago girl so her heart will always be in the deep dish.

"why won't you even try?"

she was refraining from biting into the giant slice on her plate, so i knew this was serious.

"he doesn't like me, there's nothing for me to try for."

of course i immediately stuffed my face, i wasn't about to let my food get cold b/c of damien.

"he's tough to get in w/ but once you do he's great."

"i'm not saying he's not great. he's just not into me and i'm not going to force it. you shouldn't either."

i managed to get her to stay at mine that night since i'd had class and worked that day, but the next day we both had off so we got a boozy brunch. marco's has bottomless mimosas, where you pay $15 and get free refills on mimosas all afternoon. it sounds like an amazing deal and it is, but when you're in your late 20s and drinking that much your body doesn't handle it well. especially when you then decide to go to a bar afterward and continue drinking. when i was first in college and would do things like that i could wake up the next day, have a little hair of the dog and be fine. now it took me three full days to recover.

but that night it didn't matter, we barhopped from st. felix to mother-lode to probably somewhere else that i can't remember. we hit all the gay bars—all the gay male bars, that is. since the palms closed and truck stop disbanded, there aren't any more girls' nights in weho. and the straight girls who like to hang at the abbey do not constitute a girls' night. that's like saying when i go to the zoo i'm the same as the giraffes. not that i'd go to a zoo, they're horrible for those poor animals, but you know what i mean.

so we drank ourselves silly and were all pda by the end of the night. i suggested we go back to mine and she got real defensive real fast.

"we have to start hanging out at my place sometimes."

"it's so much quieter at mine."

"you have to try. i told you this is important to me."

i think we fought a little bit more, i don't really remember because of the booze, but we ended up going back to her place. i always get pretty handsy when i'm drunk so i just wanted to have sex w/ her by that point.

we got back to her place and went straight to her room. we started kissing and undressing and then i heard it. i stopped to listen to be sure while she kept kissing me, and i was sure.

damien was having sex w/ some trick in his room and they were super loud.

"that's disgusting." i pulled back from b.

"what?" she listened for only a second and heard it. "oh."

i looked for my shirt and started getting dressed. "i can't believe you made me come here."

b sat up, still in bed but not committing to getting out. "made you come here? this is where i live."

"yeah w/ that disgusting pig. and now i have to listen to him have sex w/ some random dude."

she stayed in bed as i pulled my bottoms up. "he's not disgusting."

"it's disgusting that he's having sex in the room next door while we're here."

my voice was getting louder but i didn't care. i hoped he heard me.

"we were about to do the same thing! and we did it w/ him here last time."

i couldn't believe she compared the magic we make in bed to the degradation across the hall. "it's different."

"you just don't like him, that's why it's different."

"he's never been nice to me."

"you haven't given him a chance." she had an answer for everything.

"why are you always defending him?"

"i'm not." she sounded defensive.

"do you defend me to him when he talks about me?"

"of course. but he doesn't talk about you like this."

i literally lol-ed. "yes he does. there's no way he has anything nice to say about me."

"he does! he thinks you're interesting."

"don't lie to me."

"don't accuse me of lying."

"whatever. i'm going to sleep on the couch."

her eyes looked like a child who was just told they could never have their favorite treat again.

"why?"

"b/c now i'm tired and angry and i just want to go to sleep."

i have a short fuse when i'm drunk and make impulse decisions. i grabbed one of the pillows and stalked out.

when i woke up the next morning i was the first one awake. my head felt like someone put a severe weather warning on my brain—high pressure, really cloudy and pounding thunder. i stumbled into the kitchen for some water and barely tried to find some advil {tbh i just opened the cabinet next to the glasses and when they weren't sitting right in front of me i gave up}.

i Frankenstein-ed my way to the bathroom and stopped b/t the bedroom doors. apparently i'd left b's open when i threw myself on the couch and she either neglected to close it or consciously chose not to. she was asleep on her side, back to the door. she snored quietly, which may have been cute some other time but w/ a hangover i just wanted to tape her nose and mouth shut.

damien's door was closed. i tried to listen to see if he was awake but quickly lost interest. continuing on to the bathroom, i peed and decided that to survive this current state i needed to just leave. doing my best not to make noise i put on my shoes and went home.

that was not a good decision. b was furious. she said i abandoned her, how could i leave w/out saying goodbye or even a note. she said i clearly wasn't serious about our relationship, was she just some trick to me? it was bad.

and i know it was my fault, i shouldn't have just up and left her, but again i make impulse decisions when i'm drunk. i apologized profusely, many many many MANY times, and i spent a long time making it up to her. she didn't emotionally blackmail me but i love her so wanted her to know it was just a stupid mistake. i brought her flowers, took her out to a nice dinner at eveleigh up on sunset, the normal i'm-sorry-i-was-a-jerk relationship stuff.

she eased up after about a week but i knew the real test was coming.

we'd had dinner at taste on melrose, i was still wiping butter off my hands from the soggy bread on a perfect grilled cheese and tomato sandwich when b started.

"let's stay at my place tonight."

i really didn't want to but i knew i couldn't argue too much. she would've immediately thrown it back in my face. i tried to casually pass on it w/ "oh really? i thought you wanted to go out tonight?"

she jumped right on that. "do you still have something against staying at mine?"

"i never had anything against it." i knew i had to be quick to respond.

"you seemed to last time."

keeping my cool, i wrapped my left hand around her right one. "i just thought you wanted to do something else tonight."

"i don't."

she didn't let go. that was a good sign.

"ok that's fine."

my bed was made. and it was across the hall from damien's.

"good. thank you."

she squeezed my hand, and i stealthily took a deep preparatory breath.

what happened when we got there can only be described as serendipity. if i were more shallow i would've gloated but that would've been rubbing b's nose in it.

she opened the door to her place and the first thing we see is this completely naked guy standing in the living room w/ a glass of water. his name was robbie, damien was kind of seeing him/just having sex w/ him all the time. b hated him, he made her angrier than i've ever seen. so much angrier than when i left that morning. i don't think he was around for v long, maybe just a couple of months, but anytime we saw him or his name came up b would fume.

as we stood there w/ his junk full on in our face he just stared at us, not in shock that we walked in on him naked but almost confused. like he couldn't figure out what we were doing there.

i could feel b's rage when she saw him.

"you could put on some fucking clothes."

i was surprised she held back so much, b/c i know she wanted to really curse him out.

he just walked to damien's room and b shut the door behind me.

damien came right out and just said, "oh hey."

that sent b into an explosion.

"oh hey? i just walked in on your naked fuckboy dripping jizz all over the living room and all you say is oh hey?"

"he's not a fuckboy, you know that."

b stepped further into the room but i stayed close to the door. i wasn't about to get in this line of fire.

"i don't care, why is he naked in my living room?"

"this isn't your living room, it's our living room."

"whatever. why is he out here naked?"

"he was getting water, he was thirsty or something."

"yeah he's always thirsty. he's the definition of thirsty. i'm tired of you always bringing him around and fucking him and him being naked on everything. it's disgusting. you're disgusting."

i snuck around them so i could watch from the hallway. it was pretty epic but i didn't need to be in the middle of it.

robbie came out from damien's room, dressed this time, and stood beside me. listening to b tear into him while he was right there made me feel a little bad for the guy. i didn't know him that well except for what b told me {and since she absolutely hated him her opinions might not be based on total accuracy} so i'm not sure if he deserved my pity. but he seemed genuinely hurt by what she said so i felt for him.

damien finally came over and said, "you should go."

he walked him to the door and half-heartedly kissed his cheek. that made me feel even worse for the guy. he was clearly into damien for whatever reason, and damien couldn't shut the door fast enough. i hope he was smarter than he seemed. i hope he realized what a bad egg damien was and moved on.

this little episode turned out to be my savior. b never pushed to stay at her place again. i don't know that it created a divide between the two of them, but it certainly shook their relationship. i think the divide really came when we moved in together. when we first started talking about it i asked b how she was going to tell damien. i knew it was going to be an ordeal for her.

we were at my place post-coital. my head faced hers while she looked up at the ceiling.

"i don't know. i'll probably just spring it on him. surprise! i'm moving out."

"why won't you tell him ahead of time?"

i watched her face furrow and wrinkle as she thought through all the scenarios.

"you know he won't take it well, that's why you asked how i'm going to tell him. he'll freak out and probably try to talk me out of it."

i turned away from her, looking up at the ceiling myself.

"and you'll probably listen."

"no i won't. i want to move in w/ you."

she took my hand in hers to emphasize her point.

"i believe that, but you always get persuaded by what he says."

"i do not."

i turned back to her.

"really? then how'd you end up w/ those $400 persol sunglasses?"

"i needed a nice pair of sunglasses and they look good on me."

"and damien convinced you to buy a $400 pair of glasses."

"i can think for myself."

"usually you can. but when damien's around it's like he's the Puppet Master."

now she turned to face me.

"so why do you think i should tell him ahead of time then? if i'm just going to bend to his every whim."

she smiled, thinking she'd bested me.

i smiled knowing i had the best retort.

"because it's time for you to stand up to him."

she didn't. again her complete avoidance of any confrontation stopped her from saying anything until the week we were moving in.

i actually can't believe he didn't pick up on it sooner though, we were packing at her place on and off for at least a month. damien's a lot of things but i never thought he was stupid.

it was the tues before we moved in that he finally noticed. we'd just finished packing up her collection of mugs {don't ask, she started when she was in high school and accumulated something like 50 or 60 mugs. we basically have an entire cabinet just for her mugs} and i was taping the box shut when he walked in.

"oh thank god, are we finally getting rid of all those?"

i didn't say anything. b looked like she was trying to will herself out of the room.

"uh, yeah."

"what're you doing w/ them, donating them?"

"sure."

he stood in the doorway, looking at both of us. "what do you mean, sure?"

i was frozen. i gripped the tape gun like it was my means of salvation. b kept her hand on the box.

"i mean, we're donating them to our new apartment."

i think damien's eyes actually caught fire. i definitely felt the temperature in the kitchen increase.

"whose new apartment." it wasn't a question, it was a threat.

"lilypad and mine."

it was so silent i think time stopped. they both stared at me and all i

84

could do was finish taping the box. the tape gun made the loudest screech but i don't think damien even heard it.

"when are you two moving in together?"

he wouldn't stop staring at me.

"this weekend."

her voice sounded so small and far away it was like i was falling down a well. i began to feel a little unsafe being around damien right then, so i picked up the box and took it into b's room.

i sat on b's bed and listened to them argue. it was pretty muffled through all the walls, but i caught damien shout, "you didn't even bother to tell me you're moving out?" as i walked out of the kitchen. b of course apologized and said she didn't know how to tell him, and he raged about how he's going to pay the rent on his own. i think she offered to help w/ the payments until he found a new roommate, which he did not take well b/c i v clearly heard him shout, "i don't want a new fucking roommate."

there were a couple more back and forths until i heard him slam his door, then b walked in zombie-style.

"you ok?"

"let's just finish up."

she walked back out of the room and all i could do was follow.

i didn't see damien at all during the move. b didn't say anything about it so i figured he was intentionally staying away. i don't know what went down b/t them on the days b/t him finding out and us moving out, she never told me and i never wanted to ask. but whatever it was kept them from talking for about 3 months.

at first i was stoked, i thought we could finally get some distance from him. but b was so sullen so much that i couldn't take joy in it for long. no matter how much i couldn't stand to be around him she needed him.

b's a wonderful person and i love her madly, but she has a difficult time getting close to ppl so she doesn't have many friends. the ones she does have she keeps v close and is immensely loyal to, and damien's the most pivotal.

she'd moved to la only a few months before she met him and i don't think she found anyone she clicked w/ before him. so when they connected she was really in need of companionship, and when you throw in how much he helped her feel secure in her identity you've got an impenetrable friendship. which wouldn't be an issue if he weren't a narcissistic man child.

even still, i could tell that she needed her friend.

we were home on the couch one night after dinner and she was flipping aimlessly through the channels, sulking as usual. i was about to give in and start the conversation to suggest that she reach out to damien when her phone buzzed.

"damien just text me."

jerk knew what i was about to do and had to beat me to the punch.

"wow really? what'd he say?"

"hey it's been a while, wanna catch up?"

she stared at her screen as if it were going to continue.

i waited a beat to see if it would. it didn't.

"are you gonna write him back?"

"well yeah. kinda rude not to."

she kept staring, her thumb nervously flicking the bottom of the phone case on and off.

"what're you gonna say?"

"yeah, i guess. i mean, it has been a while."

"and you've missed him."

"yeah. i mean...yeah."

she wrote him back and they made a plan to meet up later that week. living w/ someone you can tell how even the smallest things change their mood, and this definitely perked her up. the next night she was really frisky and playful, she wanted to get dessert after dinner another night. it was like we were in vacation mode.

they went out for dinner the night they met up. b invited me out of politeness and i politely declined, which i'm pretty certain she was secretly happy about.

i put on my pink comfy sweatpants that she hates and ate a frozen vegan pizza w/ a negroni while watching *How to Get Away With Murder.* it was glorious.

when b finally got home she was buzzed—both in the tipsy sense and in the way-too-much-energy sense.

"oh my god you're not gonna believe this."

she barely shut the door before blurting it out.

i paused the 4th episode of HTGAWM i was on.

"are you drunk?"

she plopped on the couch next to me.

"no! maybe. a little."

"were you drinking martinis?"

"fine, yes. but only two. ok three."

i love drunk b, she's hilarious. i laughed at her.

"it's fine."

"i know. but you are not gonna believe this."

she grabbed my hand with both of hers in excitement.

"in the past 3 months damien's weaseled his way into a promotion, met a new guy, broke up w/ said new guy then got back together w/ him, and may have accidentally insulted smg."

she paused for dramatic effect. or to figure out which of me in her blurred vision was the actual me. i couldn't tell.

"i...have a lot of questions."

"i know right. let's start w/ the most important, obviously."

"obviously smg."

"of course. so he posted this throwback from *Buffy* season 1 where she's got the knee high boots, cute mini dress and i-just-got-fucked-in-the-car hair—"

"my fave."

"i know right. i miss the 90s. so he posts it and is like tb to my teenage crush before i knew i was gay, and he gets all these likes and this fan page comments such a great pic thanks for posting. so damien writes back my pleasure, always love seeing my girl in her heyday when she was relevant, totally joking, and the fan page totally freaks out on him. they say how can you say that about her, you don't really love her, and they get in this total feud. then he realizes, oh shit what if this is actually smg?"

she was starting to lose me, mostly b/c i don't find sarah michelle gellar all that interesting.

"i thought it was a fan account?"

"it was, but you know how celebs sometimes use their own fan accounts."

to my surprise, she was completely serious.

"do they?"

"of course! a lot of them set up fake ones so they can search themselves w/out anyone knowing."

"i don't think that's accurate."

she discarded my dissent. "so he replies again and apologizes, but doesn't want to point out that it might be smg b/c he doesn't want to scare her off."

i knew i had to play along. "right, b/c then she might never talk to him again."

"exactly. so he apologizes but she never responded."

"so she probably still won't ever talk to him again?"

"yeah. sucks."

her eyes started to get sleepy.

"well at least he may have had some interaction w/ her through the internet and her fake fan account that she may or may not have created as a front to cyber-stalk herself, which is more than a lot of ppl can say."

"yeah."

she had nestled her head into my lap by that point and was moving from drunk b to passed out b.

it was sweet, i have to admit, to see how happy she was to have her friend back. their new-found relationship became less codependent than it was before, which made me happy.

damien didn't warm up to me anymore but it wasn't as much of an issue since they weren't living together. he came over to our place a couple of times, then he bought this house in the hills and we went over there a couple times.

the whole situation w/ his house was a little sketchy and i never felt totally comfortable there. he'd had this insane boss at work, and again i hate using terms of mental illness as casual negative descriptors but from the stories he told she seemed to have legit mental problems.

he said the company paid for her to go to anger management counseling but after a few months the counselor told the company not to waste their money, she was basically a lost cause. and i guess she would verbally and physically accost him, according to him.

i have my doubts about the physical assaults. i feel like if that were to actually happen it'd be an immediate dismissal regardless of the situation. also damien's prone to exaggerating and often blatant lying. he tells everyone he moved to la for the weather when in actuality he came here to "make it", as they say.

i understand why he'd lie, he failed at his dream and was devastated by it. b actually met him the day it all fell to pieces.

he was drinking himself silly at truck stop when she bumped into him. he'd been on his tenth or so meeting w/ a prospective agent who not-so gently told him he should just give it up and go home. so he took this job as a means for survival, which created a lot of bitterness toward the job itself and aggression toward his boss.

and trust, i understand not liking your job. i've worked in hotels for way too long, and even a nice one like the one i'm at still tests my patience on the daily. the entitlement ppl have is legit shocking, and their behavior toward others they perceive as "beneath them" is flat out offensive. but that's why i'm back in school. i'm trying to get myself out of this situation, rather than take out my disappointment on everyone who's stuck in the situation w/ me.

so the company gave him a big settlement for whatever cruelty he endured and fired her. now i'd never support any form of abuse and i always believe the victim, but in this case the victim was damien.

he made it seem like he'd goad her, which combined with his flair for the dramatic makes his testimony highly suspect. anytime he spoke about her he always sang that 80s song "come on eileen", so i know he said it to her more times than he should've. and while i've never met her, that stupid song would drive anyone crazy so i'm sure it antagonized her.

on top of that he said he'd always tease her about being a lesbian b/c he knew it aggravated her. firstly that's really childish behavior, and secondly it's terrible to weaponize sexuality as a means to bully someone. especially for a gay man who no doubt spent his youth being mocked for his own sexuality. granted i don't know for sure that damien was made fun of, but i think it's a pretty safe assumption.

and then he'd been dating this new guy who's name i can never remember—his family was from sri lanka so it was something south asian. i thought he was indian at first but b was quick to correct me. i feel really dumb admitting this but i didn't know sri lanka was considered part of asia. i probably couldn't point it out on a map tbh.

but they'd been dating for a while and even living together at damien's apartment, but then when damien got the house he broke up w/ him. the guy seemed harmless, pretty bland and not that interesting to me, but he was insanely attractive so I figured that's why damien was dating him. i'm not one to fawn over guys but he could've been a model. we only met him once i think, since damien didn't keep him around for v long. to me it was v indicative of damien's habit of using ppl when he needs them and then throwing them away once he's done w/ them.

but whatever the sitch w/ the house, it helped keep us a little more separate from damien. it was up in laurel canyon so kind of a pain to get to, and there was zero parking. thankfully b shares my extreme hatred of having to spend hours looking for parking, so she never pushed to go up to his place.

even worse for me than the parking is all the time in the car winding up those canyon roads. i hate driving, i know that's a weird thing to say and deeply ironic living in la, but i do. everything about it is awful—the other drivers, sitting endlessly in traffic, the cars. cars are such a waste of money and need so much attention and care it's annoying. how can we be so technologically advanced and still have brand new cars that require so much maintenance? it's obnoxious.

and cars in la are the perfect microcosm representation of the classist divide in this country. you can pull up to any restaurant or store in bh and all you'll see are rolls royces, bentleys, teslas and the like, but the second a honda tries to get in they send you to the delivery entrance in the back like it's going to desecrate their precious valet.

if you're one of the few who relies on the buses or subways here then you're basically looked at as unhoused. taking public transportation in la is the equivalent of living in a 3rd world country. bh seriously has it written in their bylaws that no subway's allowed to pass through their borders. and they wonder why they're targeted by the underprivileged.

anyway. sorry for the tangent. damien and b were in a good place and then the week before the incident happened. it started on tues night.

b asked damien if he wanted to come over for dinner b/c she hadn't seen him for a while. i wasn't bothered by it b/c like i said things w/ damien had mellowed out. he told b he was exhausted from all the craziness w/ the woman he worked w/, was probably just going home to feed his cat and b understood.

when i got home from work b was still indecisive about what to do for dinner, so i suggested we check out that new restaurant conservatory on santa monica. it was a clear cool night so the walk would be nice and it'd been a while since we had a date night. i heard the food was supposed to be good, but wasn't super excited about the place itself.

it's part of this recent influx of wannabe high-end places that are springing up all along the blvd. the neighborhood's getting a lot more hetero and a lot more wealthy, so i think weho's trying to cater to that demographic {which is a whole other diatribe i could go on}. to me it feels disingenuous. they're trying to do high-end cheaply, which then looks obvious.

and i don't blame them, you can't have a super fancy experience when hamburger mary's is across the street throwing another night of drag queen bingo filled w/ screaming sorority sisters laughing at the local drag queen's quasi-inappropriate yet not-too-racy jokes. the two just don't go together.

but anyway, we decide on conservatory and of course the first person i see when we walk in is damien w/ one of his new guys. i think he said they were just friends but they were so obviously not. even if damien wasn't sleeping w/ him like he said, this guy was infatuated w/ him.

he looked a little like jonah hill circa Superbad, which does not fit into the weho scene or damien's typical dating demographic. damien pretty much only hung out w/ ppl he wanted to sleep w/, so i never quite figured out what he was doing w/ him. we'd met him a few times, his name was jacob and every time we saw him he was fawning over damien.

this night was no exception.

i really hoped b wouldn't notice them but of course she did. jacob was a sore spot for her, not quite to the extent that robbie was but close. she knew that he wasn't being honest about his feelings so she didn't trust him w/ damien. i thought she was being a bit over-protective b/c damien could take care of himself, but i guess i was proven wrong on that point.

once she saw them she walked straight to their table and started chatting w/ damien. jacob was highly annoyed at the interference. he looked at b w/ this sneer smile that gave me goose bumps.

i kept trying to sneak away but it took three or four times for b to finally notice. when we walked away jacob finally smiled as he waved us off, but i think he'd have preferred to push us away.

the rest of the night b couldn't stop watching damien. every conversation was me droning on about something while she "mmm-hmm"-ed and "oh nice"-ed her way through.

i finally leaned across the table to get her attention.

"babe let it go. he just wanted to go out w/ that guy."

she kept her head turned toward damien when she responded.

"no i know, i'm not mad about it. doesn't that guy seem weird though?"

"every guy damien's been into has been weird."

"but damien's not into him. and loverboy doesn't get it."

"it's not your problem. you can't babysit him."

"i know." she looked over at damien w/ real concern in her eyes.

i put my hand over hers. "he's fine."

she nodded and we finished eating.

when we left the restaurant the guys were still drinking. b didn't say it but i could tell she didn't want to leave damien. we walked all the way back to the apartment and as i unlocked the front gate of the building i heard her take a step back.

"i think i should check on him."

i held the gate open, really wanting to get into my pjs.

"really i'm sure he's fine."

b kept her ground.

"i just want to be sure. he was drunk when we left, and i don't trust loverboy."

i knew if i dragged her inside she wouldn't let this go.

"ok if it'll make you feel better. do you want the keys or just buzz when you get back?"

"i'll buzz you, i won't be long."

she kissed me goodbye and went on her way.

she came back about fifteen minutes later, and when she walked into the apartment she didn't look v relieved.

"is he ok?"

"yeah i think so. he's drunk, but loverboy was too so i'm sure they're fine."

we went to bed not long after.

we had an even stranger run-in that fri. we were walking to trader joe's to get some of their pre-made bellinis for brunch on saturday and we see damien's ex-boyfriend/lover/whatever he was. robbie, the one we always saw naked.

i try not to judge too much, but after only really knowing him being naked and/or having sex w/ damien and then seeing the oversized belt he tried to pass as shorts i can't help it. do the boys in weho really have to be such a stereotype? i mean, i'm sure his self-objectification is masking some deep insecurities, and normally i'd feel for someone going through that, but in the moment it was hard not to judge. plus it's jan, it's ok to put on some real clothes.

b was holding my hand as we walked and the instant she saw him her grip tensed. i didn't recognize him at first, unfortunately like i said a lot of boys in weho wear too little clothing even in jan so he didn't stand out.

he saw us too and it took a minute after locking eyes w/ b for him to put it all together. when he did his eyes grew thin and he curled into a little devil smile.

"hi b."

"fuck i thought you'd left town."

she hated him so hard.

"sorry." he didn't sound sorry. "i saw damien yesterday."

"no wonder he sounded miserable when we spoke."

he struck a pose to highlight how proud he felt.

"he wants to see me again."

"no he doesn't."

"we're getting together tomorrow."

i'm pretty sure i heard b grind her teeth.

"no you're not."

"maybe we'll get back together for good." his eyebrow cocked when he said this.

she took a step toward him, i think to feel intimidating, but didn't release my hand.

"weren't you crying in the street the last time i saw you?"

refusing to back down, he took a step toward her. it was slightly comical, since he's shorter than i am and i'm already pretty short. so b towered over him.

"no. the last time i saw you damien was fucking me all over your bed."

b's hand went cold and both our mouths dropped. his smile grew and he walked away, waving a snarky hand.

b could barely look at me.

"do you think he was serious?"

"no damien would never do that. he knows how much you hated him."

i wanted to sound reassuring but i'm not sure i nailed it. i really couldn't tell if he was lying.

we both tried to shake it off, but that little snake's venom hurt. if that was true it was beyond horrific. only a truly demonic person would go to such lengths to spite someone they considered a friend. and that's the only reason damien would've done something like that, is out of spite toward b.

she tried to call him to make sure he wasn't actually going to see robbie again. if he sank his teeth back in damien he would never let go. she never did reach him, and then we heard about this.

b was devastated of course, i've never seen her sob like that. she feels so guilty, i think she thinks robbie had something to do w/ it and she should've done more. i think it was more likely jacob out of jealousy. maybe he heard that damien ran into robbie and was afraid it would diminish his chances.

but i try not to engage w/ b on who may or may not have done it b/c it sends her spiraling. i keep telling her there was nothing else for her to do but it's hard when you lose someone that close to you. i wish i could do more but all i can do is be there for her.

THE BOSS

You're only really important if someone wants to kill you. And not some half-assed joke I-want-to-kill-you, the I'll-shoot-you-in-the-head kill you. I always told that little prick he'd never be that important. I guess he found someone more protozoan than him.

He started in our department what, three years ago? Two? I don't keep track, especially not for an incompetent weasel like him. I'd been through four other assistants in the past year and a half so HR was on me to hire someone and behave. Somehow it's my problem, I'm the one who's always held accountable. It's not their responsibility to find someone who's qualified or at the very least not a complete fuck up.

But he seemed halfway intelligent in the interview—I don't know how he was able to pull that off so well being the nimrod that he is. But he fooled me enough so I thought he was moderately capable and hired him. Biggest mistake of my career, no question.

His first week was the worst clusterfuck I've ever seen. I actually don't know how he managed to fuck things up so badly. A monkey throwing its own shit on the walls would've wreaked less havoc.

To start it off, every time he could work it in he'd shout, "Come on Eileen!" at me. And it wasn't just in the beginning. He said it every fucking day that I saw him, at least two to three times a day. He knew it drove me crazy too. That useless primate loved to push people's buttons; he'd figure out their pet peeves and work them until they break. And then when you push back on him suddenly he's the innocent one being victimized. Fucking snake.

It was his second or third day, I don't care enough to try to remember, but I had a lunch meeting and called in from the car to be connected with Jan in publicity. That moronic middle-schooler hung up on me five times. I'm not exaggerating. FIVE FUCKING TIMES.

What am I supposed to do in that situation? The first two times I kept my cool and tried to talk him through it, but after the third time I let him have it.

"If you can't even manage the fucking phones how am I supposed to trust you with a marketing campaign?"

"I'm sorry Eileen."

He didn't even sound sorry, the chromosomal defect. Looking back he might've been doing it on purpose. He's a vindictive little viper. Or was.

"Don't be sorry, be fucking smart."

My next call was to HR to get a replacement but they said I had to "give him a chance" and "allow him to grow into the position". They told me I should "mentor" him so he could be a leader for "the next generation". I'm not a fucking preschool teacher, I'm not here to educate the youth. I've got a tough fucking job and either you keep up or I kick you out.

Plus I don't give a fuck about the next generation. These fucking millenials are so lazy they're lucky anyone bothers to hire them. And if I were a man no one would ever even think about saying this bullshit to me.

In the beginning he really tried to kiss my ass. He laid it on thick too. He'd always smile ear to ear like a kid in front of his birthday cake.

"Good morning Eileen, how was your night?"

It was so disingenuous, and like I want to chit chat with him anyway.

He loved to tell anyone who'd listen how everyone thought he was an actor when he first moved here. That was one of the first things he said to me.

"Even the nice old woman who sold me my car insurance asked if I moved out here to be in 'pictures'. Who even calls them pictures anymore?" A senile old hag with no concept of reality, that's who.

The same goddamn story every time too, like he'd rehearsed it. He'd laugh this stupid fake laugh like he was in a tampon commercial. He claims he came here for the weather but that's bullshit. That attention whore was so desperate to be famous he probably killed himself just to get on the news.

The worst was when he'd try to tell me about his pitiful life.

"My roommate dragged me to this lesbian party over the weekend."

He was always fishing to find out if I'm a dyke. The gays always do that, they want you to be one of them. And no I don't have a problem with them, don't start that homophobic bullshit with me. I have nothing against any gay except this particular retarded rainbow, and that has nothing to do with his sexuality. I think the community would be happy they don't have to take credit for him anymore. My point is all of them should mind their own business when it comes to who I'm sleeping with.

So here I am stuck with a kindergarten drop out for an assistant that HR won't let me fire and I'm supposed to play nice with him. Teach him to grow. Fuck that. He couldn't grow if he was the only plant in the pot. And did anyone tell him to play nice with me? Of course not. The slack-jawed jackass had so much attitude I wanted to punch him every time I saw him.

I had a breakfast meeting one morning with the VP of Development who was in town from NY and just like always we had to have it at his hotel, which just like always is fucking Shutters on the Beach. Halfway on the other side of the planet. Our office is in Burbank and I live in Sherman Oaks, so he might as well have asked me to meet him in Vegas.

The meeting's always longer than it needs to be because the prick loves to hear himself speak, so by the time I get back to the office it's fucking noon. I'm a hundred emails behind with a million more on my to-do list, and what's my genius of an assistant doing when I rush in? Eating a fucking sandwich. Probably peanut butter and jelly too, the ignorant infant. He had the maturity level of one of those inflatable bounce houses. Have you seen the way he dressed? He always wore these stupid t-shirts with some fucking cartoon character on it like he was coming off the playground at recess.

So I say to him as I hurry by, "I need the files on the spring releases. Did Tom Dancy call?"

"No."

I could barely make it out with his mouth fucking full.

"No what?" I had to shout from behind my desk, he didn't even bother to follow me in.

"No, Tom didn't call."

I don't even think he turned his head away from that goddamned sandwich.

After waiting a minute to see if any common sense would infiltrate that thick skull, I stormed out to stand beside his desk. "Do you have the files?"

"No." He took another bite of that fucking sandwich.

I should've won an Oscar for holding back the way I did. "Why the fuck not?"

"I'm eating."

As if I couldn't tell. He basically spat half that stupid sandwich on me as he spoke.

"I don't give a shit, fucking do what I say when I fucking say it. Get me the goddamn spring release files."

Now he finally looked up at me. "It's my lunch break."

"What part of do what I fucking say when I say it don't you understand, you fucking idiot? Get me the fucking files. Now." Then he starts writing something down. "What the fuck are you writing? Unless you're personally writing the files before my very eyes, fucking stop and get me the fucking spring release files."

That brain-dead hyena took another bite of that goddamned sandwich before getting up. I could've choked the life out of him right there. This is what I had to put up with. And I couldn't fire him! Corporate bullshit.

He got more and more cocky as time went on. If fucking HR would've let me fire him from the beginning, it never would've escalated so badly. They were just lazy; they didn't want to have to start looking for candidates again so kept pushing me to make it work with that useless preschooler. He knew they didn't want me to fire him too, and giving an imbecilic vulture like that any kind of power is dangerous.

This one Friday I was completely dying—we were six weeks out on our biggest release and the fucking producers decided they didn't like the billboard designs everyone agreed upon two months ago. So I'm freaking out and as always he was sat at his desk, probably doing nothing. Actually no, he was probably photoshopping another background for his desktop with pictures of Sarah Michelle Gellar. He was obsessed with her, literally. He made this stupid fucking collage for his computer with images of her from all the horror movies she's been in. Mostly of her screaming.

That's psychotic, and misogynistic frankly. He's displaying a series of images where a woman is constantly in peril and near death to look at every day. He told me once he watches *Scream* to help fall asleep. People getting butchered soothes him; more specifically, women getting butchered. That's not normal.

But does anyone ask me how I feel about having an employee who posts pictures of terrified women all over his desk? Absolutely not, he's a man so it's all fine. He's a man by genetic definition only—intellectually and emotionally he's more in line with an XY chromed sperm that died before it penetrated an egg, but society still gives him all the fucking privileges.

Anyway, I'm in total crisis mode, running around the office like a lunatic. I hadn't eaten all day so was starving and he's doing arts and crafts at his desk. He never asked what he could do to help, never tried to figure out what I needed, he just fucking sat there. I finally lost it and shouted, "You could fucking help."

That lazy leech looked up at me like he had no idea what was going on. "With what?"

"Anything! Pick literally anything and fucking do it." That idiotic toddler looked around then just started typing. "What the fuck are you doing?"

Once again he didn't look at me when he answered. If I didn't know what a rude rodent he was, I'd say he was scared of me.

"I'm emailing Dan in HR to make sure you approved my hours."

I think I actually cut my palms with my fingernails from clenching my fists so hard. "I need you to do some actual fucking work."

He was still typing. I don't know what kind of novella he was writing, but each keystroke felt like an intentional punch to my gut.

"I am. This is on your to-do list."

My teeth clenched so hard I think I got lock-jaw. "There's a million fucking things that need to get done..."

"Come on Eileen. I'm only one man."

By this point he knew it pissed me off when he said that, and he knew exactly how to use it as a fuck you.

I couldn't hold it any longer. But can you blame me? "You're not any fucking man."

He finally stopped typing and looked me directly in the eyes. I knew he was challenging me.

"I don't think it's appropriate for you to speak to me like that."

It took every ounce of will power not to physically assault him. Still I think I was pretty restrained when I said, without shouting I might add, "I will fuck your face off."

He laughed some dumb fucking half laugh. "You definitely can't say that to me."

"I just fucking did. I will fuck your face off you entitled little prick." I didn't need to hold back anymore, he had that and a whole lot more coming to him.

He laughed that same stupid laugh and took that fucking notebook out from his drawer. What I later found out was that he'd been taking notes on everything I did that he felt was too mean toward him. He never came to me to address any problems like an adult. He compiled some list of all the ways I "wronged" him and took it to HR behind my back. He's a devious little vampire.

HR's not any better. They believe him over me, after I've been there for fifteen years. FIFTEEN FUCKING YEARS. They pulled me in for a "touch base on workplace interactions", which was basically an intervention to be nicer to fuck ups, more specifically the one they'd placed on my desk.

They told me not only that I couldn't fire that pompous parasite, but they were moving him and promoting him. AND there was a departmental dinner that everyone had to attend to celebrate, in which I was meant to "clear the air" with him.

I get reprimanded and that human waste of natural resources not only avoids any consequences for being the most inane nitwit, but gets rewarded for being a quote unquote man who had to deal with a difficult (READ: superior) woman.

At least we went to Bouchon. If I'm going to be forced to celebrate the manipulated rise of the most conniving corporate climber the food better be good. Toby, Alex and Jas were waiting at the maître d' stand when I got there; of course that deadbeat defecation wasn't there yet.

I told them to seat us, fuck waiting for him. We ordered our drinks and they were served to us before that self-important sycophant showed up with whatever hooker he could hire to be with him. No one would willfully choose to hang around that illiterate preteen.

I sat facing the entrance so when those hapless homos walked up I stared right at them. "You're late."

"It's seven-thirty now. That's when the reservations were for." He said it with a smug smirk that I wanted to slap right off his stupid face. It was at least seven forty anyway.

Celebration or not, I wasn't about to back down. "You're late."

Alex, always the peacekeeper, raised her glass. "Let's toast."

I love Alex. She's always positive, a hard worker and smarter than most of the idiots we worked with. She deserves a promotion, not that evolutionary regression.

"We don't have our drinks yet."

That daft dope doesn't deserve a toast from Alex. I certainly wasn't going to wait for him. I drank my wine.

I turned to the pumped and primped pauper the promoted pig brought with him. "So who are you?" I didn't sign on to play nice with his side piece.

His response was as intellectually stimulating as I expected. "I'm Robbie."

"What do you do, Robbie?"

He was too dumb to catch the aggression in my voice, and his stare was as blank as his brain. "I work at Motherlode."

"And what is Motherlode?"

"It's a gay bar on Santa Monica."

He was so dumb he ruined the fun of the slaughter. I grabbed my wine to lubricate the boredom of his conversation. "Of course it is. What kind of degree do they require to work there?"

He was just as stupid as his pathetic host. He snorted and said, "What?"

"I'm sure they only recruit from the most exclusive schools."

All he could respond with was, "I don't know."

I looked across the table and raised my glass to that soul-sucking bum. "Congrats, I didn't think it'd be possible for you to find someone just as stupid as you are."

He put his hand on his piglet's. How chivalrous. "You can't talk to us like that."

If his attempt at being a protector was any more comical I would've laughed hysterically. Even his failures aren't that impressive.

"I'm congratulating you, that's what we all came here to do."

"We came because of my promotion." He dug into that word, knowing it cut me deep.

"Enjoy it while you can. It won't last long." I drank my wine without breaking his stare.

"Hey all, we're here to celebrate." Alex jumped in again and I chose to follow her diversion. The messiah of morons and his disciple had gotten their prissy drinks, so had something to fill their mouths with to keep them from talking.

I decided to channel my energy elsewhere and spent the rest of the night pretending to care about Toby and his endless stories of whichever wanna be actress/singer/waitress he was fucking. Or *trying* to fuck, to be more precise. Once the food was served, the prostitute began inhaling every piece of fried chicken within his reach. It was like he'd never been to a restaurant or seen real food before. I was going to call him out on it but held my tongue to spare Alex, Toby and Jas. Mostly Alex, she was trying really hard.

The following Monday, that dimwitted dipshit started as marketing manager. How he pulled off not getting fired within the first hour is his only accomplishment in life.

At our first staff meeting, we were discussing the award season push for Benedict Cumberbatch's latest period disaster and Shit-For-Brains thought it'd be cute to dress him up in clothes for each weather season since everyone calls it "award season". IT'S NOT ABOUT THE FUCKING SEASONS YOU MORON. It took all my self-control not to stab him in the eye with my pen. But I did snap it in half under the table (thankfully I didn't get any ink on my Celine pants).

Apparently he also saw us as equals now, and thought I cared about his shitty life. That scrawny little turd had the nerve one day to walk into my office unannounced and sit down as if I was his fucking therapist.

I was in the middle of reviewing a new campaign proposal and couldn't believe when I saw him walk in. I didn't wait for him to say anything.

"I know your delusions of mediocrity lead you to believe we're on the same level, but we are not and you are not allowed to enter my office whenever you feel like it."

"I need to ask your advice." He sat back in the chair as if he was making himself at home.

"You should kill yourself."

The self-involved ignoramus ignored my advice and kept going. "So my friend B, the lesbian roommate I've told you about, she moved in with her girlfriend and things are weird between us now."

I almost crumpled the entire proposal, I got so fired up. "I don't give a shit."

And yet he still didn't get it.

"Do lesbians automatically turn on any male in their life once they get in a relationship?"

Once again I had to control myself, despite my work day being interrupted IN MY OWN OFFICE. "Get out."

He kept looking at me like he actually believed I cared. I knew he was stupid but I never realized he crossed over to delusional.

"Seriously. It's like she's forgotten our entire friendship leading up to now. I don't get it, I'm a really good friend."

I cannot stand when people say things like that. If you have to explicitly tell me that you're a good person or everyone loves you, what you're really telling me is you're a fucking asshole and no one wants to be around you. Or when people say "I'm not a gossip" and then immediately launch into the most gossipy story. Do they really think they're fooling anyone? Only themselves, I'll tell you that much.

I didn't launch into any of that with this serial fool. I just wanted him gone as quickly as possible.

"Seriously get the fuck out. Or kill yourself."

But he still didn't move.

"It's pretty obvious her girlfriend isn't my biggest fan but does that mean she has to completely abandon me?"

And once again I let go of the need to hold back. "If you don't leave, I will murder you myself and make it look like suicide."

"Did you turn on all your guy friends when you got in a relationship?"

What I really want to know is, what would anyone else do in this situation? How am I not given the right to react when this stymied yokel won't leave me alone? My response of, "I'm not a fucking lesbian" feels pretty restrained.

And his response felt like a very intentional slap in the face.

"Right. You've probably never had a lasting relationship, that's why you never had kids. Sorry."

He gave this condescending look of faux-concern, the same one every other person gives me when they find out I don't have children. Fuck him and fuck everyone else. I made a decision not to have kids and I'm fucking happy. Not having children doesn't make me any less of a person or any less of a woman, so everyone can just fuck right off.

Maybe there was a time years ago that I thought I wanted them, because as a woman we have to want children in order to be considered a woman. I don't even know if I *actually* wanted them. I'd probably be losing my shit every day and wondering why I got myself into that mess. But I CHOSE to focus on my career and in doing so CHOSE not to have children. It wasn't an accident so everyone can save their fucking pity for someone pitiful.

So then I got really pissed and stood up. "Fuck you."

He remained sat in that fucking chair like his sorry ass was glued to it.

"Hypothetically then. Would you abandon me if you found someone who'd put up with you?"

"I'll abandon you out this fucking window."

That's where it ended. He was intimidated enough to walk out of my office and that was it. He says I threw my stapler at him after I said that but I'm not dumb enough to do that. Obviously I'm going to get fired if I start throwing shit at people, and I wasn't about to lose my job over a fuckwit like him. Plus if I were going to attack him I'd go full force and use scissors.

Surprisingly he took the hint though, and never came in my office again. He still found ways to annoy me, he just did it in front of other people so he had witnesses.

We were wrapping up a staff meeting one Friday when Alex, being the amiable person she is, asked me what plans I had for the weekend.

"I've got brunch at the Beverly Hills Hotel on Sunday."

That genealogical mishap jumped right in as if he owned the conversation.

"You can't go to the Beverly Hills Hotel anymore. The Sultan of Brunei made it law that any homosexual in that country will get stoned to death. It's illegal to be gay there. Didn't you see what George Clooney said about boycotting Dorchester hotels?"

The rage I felt made me almost rip the zipper off my LV briefcase. "I don't give a fuck what George Clooney said. I go there every Sunday for brunch, I'm not changing my plans for him or anyone else."

He stood across the table trying to look at me like an equal.

"It's inhumane what they're doing, you can't support them."

"I'm supporting the people who work at the Beverly Hills Hotel, not you or George Clooney or the fucking Sultan of Brunei."

"You are supporting the Sultan though, indirectly. That's George Clooney's point."

"Fuck George Clooney. I don't care and don't pretend you do either. You're just a fucking sheep."

My pen had run out of ink so I threw it toward the garbage can, but lo and behold it hit that walking trashbag square in the chest.

"Ow, don't be such a bitch."

He gripped his chest like I shot an arrow at him. I knew he was weak and I was pitcher for our college softball team, but it couldn't have hurt that much.

Still I threw my bag down on the table. "A bitch? Fuck you and your pencil dick, who the fuck do you think you are?"

"Everyone else here acts like normal people, why can't you?"

"Everyone else can fuck right off, I don't give a shit about you or the Sultan of fucking wherever."

"Fuck you." He tried to sound intimidating. He sounded more like a Disney star throwing a tantrum.

"FUCK YOU. Next time I'll actually try to hit you and aim for your fucking head."

For the record, I was not intentionally trying to hit him in that moment.

If I were, why the fuck would I throw a pen? What damage could that possibly do? And again how dumb would I be to do that in front of everyone?

Two weeks later—maybe three, maybe a month, I don't know or remotely care—Toby and I were wrapping up the layouts for some garbage kids' release we got stuck with and were about to leave for the night. We were packing up and he mumbles, "Man, can you believe Damien?"

"What'd the Sultan of Stupidity do now?"

He leaned in to whisper, as if someone else might hear. We were the only ones in the room.

"He didn't do anything, he's completely tore up. Didn't you hear him crying in the bathroom?"

I didn't keep my voice down. "No, why doesn't anyone call me when these things happen? I could've used a pick-me-up today."

"He was sobbing in one of the toilets, but then I heard him whisper-screaming into his phone. He's all over the place."

"He's a lunatic, I told you."

"Alex thinks he got dumped."

"Any person with half a brain would dump that pile of shit."

"What if he's really hurting?"

"Then hopefully he'll drive off the road on Mulholland and end his woes. Finally make this world a better place."

"What if he does something crazy?"

"Then I'll be the first to turn him in."

He didn't do anything crazy, as far as I know. But he was a fucking pill, moreso than usual. He moped around the office like his dick got cut off and it's all anyone wanted to talk about. "Do you think he's sick?", "Maybe one of his parents died?", "I heard he lost his cat", "Does he have parents?" Everyone loves the gossip. I couldn't be bothered so didn't hear much about the details. He did come in with a black eye one day and I laughed at him.

"You probably got that from a newborn."

"Fuck off." He walked away pretty quickly, which was unusual for him.

I gave him a pass because it was too funny. I can't imagine that Ice Capades reject in a fight—he'd probably just flail and cry immediately. Alex heard some guy did it to him, probably some trashbag he picked up in a bar who finally realized what a fuck up he is.

I shouldn't have let him off so easy though, because two weeks later he gave me the royal fuck. I should've anticipated it, but I didn't give the sneaky little cretin enough credit. I didn't think he had balls at all, let alone the balls to do this.

My good friend Dan in HR called me into his office on a Friday morning. For those who don't know corporate, that's never a good time for HR to want to see you. I went straight there after parking and he's sat behind his desk all proper with paperwork laid out in front of him.

Dan waited for me to sit before he began.

"Eileen, you know we've had some complaints about your behavior toward coworkers."

"Just tell me what this is."

"It's come to our attention that you've continued verbally abusing other staff and it's escalated to physical assaults—"

"That's bullshit, who have I physically assaulted?"

"—so we have to terminate you, effective immediately."

"That's fucking bullshit, who said I assaulted them?"

Dan looked at me blankly.

It was complete bullshit. I know for a fact at least a dozen male execs who'd done exactly what I did, if not worse—one actual physical fight with punches and choking in the lobby—and the worst they got was a suspension. If I'd been a man this all would've gone entirely different. I probably would've been able to fire the calcified caveman from the start, and definitely never would've been fired over his word. At worst I would've been suspended like those other pricks.

Everyone's shouting that Me Too bullshit all over town but nothing's changed. What about ME FUCKING TOO? Who's protecting me and the other women trying to break the mold in this corporate fucking frat house?

No wonder the organization went to shit. They throw Witherspoon and Aniston a few producing credits and think they're changing the fucking world. I bet every development exec who greenlit their bullshit was a fucking man, there wasn't a single woman in any of those meetings. They all thought it would make them look good so they wouldn't have to do any heavy lifting, which is what we need if we want real change. Instead of getting in bed with Cuomo when he's inevitably charged with sexual assault, why don't you help some of us on the inside push these perverts out? I had to fight my way in, not just to the top but even to have a chance to play the game. Then this worthless mongrel gets handed the keys to the kingdom just because he was born with the better genitalia. Giving a few high profile women opportunities for optics isn't progress, it's showmanship.

But Dan wouldn't answer my question, which I knew he wouldn't but he should've. He didn't have to though, I knew exactly which back-stabbing pariah did this.

"I need you to sign these."

He pushed some papers toward me and I pushed them right off his desk.

"I'm not signing anything, you'll hear from my lawyers."

I went to leave and wouldn't you know, two staff security guards were waiting to escort me out.

I know that genetic wasteland told them I assaulted him, I know he put together an entire HR case against me. He's an entitled little prick and he knew as long as I was there, he'd never manipulate his way to the top of the ladder.

If I'd seen him then I would've killed him right on the spot. But thankfully for us both, I haven't seen him since before I was fired, so I didn't kill him. But goddamn, I'd like to shake the hand of whoever did.

THE OTHER EX-BOYFRIEND

It isn't too much of a wonder that Damien died. He couldn't have lived past forty anyway, he would've been a terrible geriatric. He's been infantilized his entire life so unable to mature beyond a pre-pubescent girl. I'm amazed he even made it as far as he did. The moment he hit the legal drinking age, he should've been dead. Not solely based on the sheer volume of alcohol he excessively consumed, which easily could've killed a person thrice his size, but more because he lacked any ability to behave like an adult. I told him this repeatedly so it's no surprise.

I met Damien...oh it's embarrassing, I really shouldn't admit to it. Unfortunately for me I'm a terrible liar so it's worthless for me to try. I met Damien on Grindr. It's so typical, I hate being such a stereotype. But here we are. I hate the bars in West Hollywood, it's even more tragic to live and breathe that scene than it is to go hunting somewhere as pedestrian as a hookup app. I mean after the ninth time of seeing that pathetic Aaron Schock out at Chapel essentially begging to get in my pants, I grew weary of treading on those sidewalks. It's such a waste too, if Aaron had any personality other than the common self-hating homo he'd be the ultimate catch. Aren't we bored of that story anyway? You're rich and you're attractive and, most importantly in this country, you're white, so get over it and suck a dick already. Nobody cares. He certainly seemed eager to. He somehow always appeared lurking in a dark corner waiting for me, basically on his knees with his mouth gaping, ready to fellate.

After being turned off by the lechers of Santa Monica Boulevard but still having a libido that needed tending to, I debased myself enough to download the app and, to my surprise, it proved quite resourceful. Damien wasn't the first guy I chatted with, or met up with for that matter. But he was the most enthusiastic, shall we say. (Kindness prevents me from calling him desperate.)

I was dating someone else at the time who was incessantly boring. I thought we had an open relationship but at the end when I told him about the other guys I'd been sleeping with, his anger surprised me, so apparently he wasn't as aware of our openness as I thought. It was fine, the relationship had been dead for months so his anger allowed him to move on without complications. He did strike me across the face though, which I could've lived without.

Damien was one of the better lays I had off Grindr so I agreed to see him more than once. I think that's more telling of the pool of men on the app as opposed to an endorsement of Damien's own skills. Everyone thinks they're great in bed but very few actually are. One guy gave me such a bad blow job that I actually made him stop and leave. After feeling teeth grind against my penis, I lost my arousal and my patience. There's nothing worse than wasting your time and energy on a bad lay, of which there are many in this city.

But Damien was comparatively pretty good, which again may have more to do with the other tricks I held him up against than his own sexual prowess. He would get a little desperate sometimes, trying to be overtly macho during the act then afterward asking me how good it was. If he was laying on the bed and I was on top, he'd put both hands under his head, flexing his biceps with a self-satisfied grin. I think he fancied himself a porn star because he was always trying to show off, often to himself. Sadly what he didn't realize is that he had no biceps to speak of, so what he deemed a flex in reality appeared more like a deflated balloon. He never had much self-awareness about how tacky he could be.

I quickly realized that his interest in me extended beyond the bedroom. He began furiously texting me on the daily, waking me with digital love notes like, "Morning handsome" with a winky-faced smile emoji (so trite in its attempt to be cute) and a continuous barrage of lame come-ons. "Woke up dreaming of you", "Wish I was having you for lunch", "I want to taste you again" etc etc. And he always wrote just the letter "u" instead of spelling out the entire word. How much longer does it take to type those extra two letters? Is it that much of an inconvenience? It's not a matter of time, he's not that busy—trust me I know. I didn't respond to all his texts, since I already had one relationship wearing me down I didn't need a second to do the same. But I admit, his enthusiasm was endearing, and I found it charming to be around someone so oblivious to his own ridiculousness. The swagger he thought he had, the faux-machismo persona he adopted were so transparent, but he embraced them so fully.

Around the third or fourth time we hooked up, he suggested we go out to dinner before we had sex. I rolled my eyes at the thought of a date but I happened to skip lunch that day so he caught me at the right time. He suggested we go to Café D'Etoile on Santa Monica—of course he'd think to go to a place that basic. It's nestled amidst all the gay bars so you get a clear view of the queens parading and peacocking for each other. The restaurant promotes itself as fancy because they have tablecloths and use linen napkins, but the food is interchangeable with Hamburger Mary's or even McDonald's if they served Americanized Italian.

I redirected to Norah, which had opened up a while ago on the opposite end of the boulevard. It's the epitome of chic. It has a gorgeous redecorated bar in the middle of the restaurant that's all white marble, and every inch is tastefully done. A far cry from the tragedy that was in that space before them, Don't Tell Mama. Oh god, that was horrendous. It looked like they went dumpster diving for all their tables and chairs. And they thought having a grand piano would somehow elevate the restaurant? Please. All it did was encourage subpar performers to sing in public.

But Norah would appease Damien's need to be amongst the common fags, and I could at least get an adequate meal. I should've been more concerned about running into Mark—that's the guy I was dating—but I figured if I did I could just lie, or honestly tell him the truth, at that point I didn't care much.

So Damien and I went on our "date" and he played it all sexy cool. He leaned back in his chair like James Dean, left arm thrown over the back nonchalantly but very purposefully planned out. His right leg crossed over the left in that lazy manner, his foot tapping against the table leg giving away his anxiety. That was always his tell; he could never sit still whenever he was the least bit agitated. I watched him in amusement as he recapped how great his day was winning over his psychotic boss, desperate to impress me. I met each of his cues with the appropriate response: "Wow, that's amazing" and "I can't believe you did that, congratulations", knowing that each stroke of his ego I'd get reciprocated in bed. It was an easy game to play but fun nonetheless.

It got more complicated once he stopped playing and bought into us for real. A few weeks in, he caught me by surprise when he asked, "When are you going to break up with Mark?"

We were at his apartment and had just finished having sex. I was midway through pulling my pants up and froze I was so taken aback.

"Why would you ask that?"

He rolled on his side to face me. "Because I want us to be together."

It may sound callous but I honestly never thought about the two of us in a relationship. Not even that I didn't want it; I had truly not given it one thought. Now apparently I had to consider it so I sat back on the bed.

His finger traced my spine in an attempt to reinforce whatever connection he thought we had. Or more to the point, what he wanted us to have.

"Don't you want that?"

I didn't turn to face him. Not to be rude, but I was just thinking it through. "I don't know."

"You don't love Mark."

At this I turned my head, but kept seated as I was. I didn't want to lead him on. "That's not the question."

His finger made it to the waist of my pants. He thought he was being coy with his sexual manipulation.

"But why stay with him?"

"My staying with him and you wanting to be in a relationship with me are two completely separate topics. One has nothing to do with the other."

He pulled his hand away, probably thinking that depriving me of his touch would send me over the edge. Poor thing.

"Not nothing. You can't be in a relationship with me if you're still in one with him."

"True."

I did like him more than Mark, but that's not saying much. Mark and I had been together four and a half years and I could not remember what I found the least bit interesting about him. When he spoke it was as if someone permanently muted him, I couldn't even hear him anymore.

Impulsively I decided to do it. I went home that night and told Mark I'd met someone and the fury ensued. There was screaming and name calling, it was all very unfortunate and base. It was a side of Mark I don't remember seeing before, and I must admit I was impressed by it. I didn't think he had that kind of strength in him. My jaw wasn't expecting it either.

Needless to say Mark kicked me out, and I acquiesced to avoid any further drama. I followed with another impulse decision that, in retrospect, was even more ill-advised than breaking the news to Mark the way that I did. I moved in with Damien. He had a second bedroom available since his former roommate moved in with her girlfriend and he couldn't be bothered to find a new one.

I thought having the separate bedrooms would push us more toward the roommate aspect as opposed to the live-in dating, but I was woefully incorrect. Damien immediately latched on to us as a couple. All he needed was a string of pearls and a day dress to complete his happy homemaker identity. The first night after I moved in I took a shower to wash the day off, and when I got out he'd dimmed all the lights, put out a few candles and somehow made us dinner. To be fair my showers can be a little lengthy, but still not long enough to prepare an entire meal without me knowing.

He stood by the table with a massive grin like he couldn't wait for me to tell him what a good job he'd done. He always needed that validation. We started eating and the chewy chicken seemed to mock me.

"I have to confess I didn't make this."

"That's good." I had difficulty enunciating through the rubbery mastications.

"I ordered from Café D'Etoile."

Of course he did. He somehow didn't catch that my initial refusal to patronize them on our first "date" was intentional. Apparently he didn't realize how mediocre the food was. He paired it with a decent red wine at least, and after dinner we enjoyed some better-than-usual sex. I guess falsifying a relationship served him well.

His eating habits were always questionable. Anything deep fried was like candy to him, and I've never seen someone consume pasta as much as he did. As a result he was always a little on the chubby side. Not fat per se, which I found surprising every time I watched him eat. But he definitely had a ring of fat around his stomach. Over time I was able to introduce him to healthier choices—it sounds ridiculous but I had to convince him to eat vegetables! And I insisted he start working out. No matter how well you eat, if you're not pushing yourself at the gym or in an exercise class, you're wasting your time. You might as well give in and eat all the terrible foods you're keeping from yourself.

Once he got in better shape (note I didn't say good shape—from where he started off, getting better did not get him anywhere near good), our situation continued on fairly well. We lived easily together for the most part, we never really had much of an argument. He could be annoying, like when he would go on one of his movie rants. He loved movies and movie trivia, which I don't care much about, but he never seemed to grasp that about me. He'd ramble on about how this movie bombed or that one should've won the Oscar. And he was obsessed with this actress Sarah Michelle Gellar. I'm not using obsessed as hyperbole either—he was clinically obsessed. He had her movie posters all over the apartment, a collection of I think all of her movies on DVD and an excess of useless information on her. Did you know she was the frontrunner to play a character named Amber in a movie called *Clueless*? I wish I didn't, but I do. I'd never heard of her or seen anything she was in, and after placating him by agreeing to one of her movies called *Suburban Girl*, I didn't feel inclined to watch more.

One of the pleasant surprises I found when moving in with him was how quickly I connected with his cat Stanley Kowalski. I never cared much about animals before—they smell, they're noisy and you have to clean up their excrement. Where's the enjoyment in any of that? Before I lived there Stanley Kowalski kept to himself when I was over, and once I became a permanent fixture he eyed me with suspicion. As I unpacked my room, he sat in the hallway outside my door staring at me. He didn't try to come in and interrupt all my business. He just watched from afar. And when I'd sit in the living room or kitchen, he wouldn't come up to me and beg for my attention. He'd sit at a distance to watch me, curious but not necessarily approving. He wasn't automatically impressed by me and I respect that. Damien seemed to think we were instantly a nuclear family. He really latched on to the idea of our relationship.

And suddenly I found myself in a complete relationship. We were a "we"—everything was "what should we have for dinner tonight", "should we get this new chair", "what are we going to do for the holidays". We were no longer individuals but a duo who apparently operated as a singular unit.

He insisted I meet his friend Jacob early on. Clearly he wanted to show me off, he was so excited about it but who can blame him. Jacob was someone he met at work I think, or maybe they met out at a bar? I can't remember, I know he told me but it wasn't that interesting.

Jacob was the type of person you keep around to feel better about yourself. There's nothing wrong with him, per se—there's just nothing great about him. He's not *un*attractive, but he's definitely not attractive. He's one of those fat people who carries his weight well—not one of those monstrosities who needs to be dragged out of their home on a forklift. I'm sure he identifies as a bear, or whatever they call themselves these days. All those identifiers are so tedious to keep track of. You're a bear, you're an otter, you're a penguin—who cares? He's a short rotund gay man who jabbers on endlessly. I'd call him a nuisance.

For our big introduction Jacob came over to *our* apartment for a "hang". Damien loved to use colloquialisms to sound cool. Or more to the point, what he thought sounded cool. Jacob came in wearing cargo pants and what I imagine was a hoodie he scrounged up from Out of the Closet, the local thrift store that benefits AIDS research. While their intentions are honorable I suppose, their clothing stock is more reminiscent of a trash heap. We ordered dinner from Granville, because who doesn't love a chain restaurant. Jacob certainly did, it was his grand idea. Maybe next time we can try Applebee's or Red Lobster. Perchance to dream.

As we were eating our mass-produced food they decided to watch some movie they've both seen a number of times. Something punch. *Suck and Punch* maybe? I don't know. I don't understand why you'd watch the same movie multiple times. It's literally hours of your life wasted. Most aren't even that good. This was just a bunch of girls fighting in different CGI landscapes. It basically looked like a video game but you didn't have the ability to control the characters. And the story didn't even make sense. They were in a home for girls but needed to defeat these fantasy sequences to get out? I probably missed some important moment of revelation during one of the many instances where my mind wandered someplace more interesting.

Jacob tried to make pleasant conversation during our "hang" but he's woefully unskilled. It was all the mundane "where are you from", "what do you do", "where'd you go to school", as if my identity were linked to my resume. I'm sure he told me the same details about himself but I either ignored him or forgot.

It was clear that he was intimidated by me, so his nerves may have gotten the best of him. He giggled like a schoolgirl at everything I said, even when I was making a direct statement not meant to be funny, and anytime he asked a question he would avert his eyes quickly when I responded. It would've been cute on a child who had a crush, but on an adult it's just pathetic.

It was so obvious that poor Jacob wanted me, I'm actually surprised Damien never got upset with him. Damien was quite possessive, especially knowing how many guys take an interest in me. Jacob wasn't subtle about his affection for me either. At one point in the night he grabbed my bicep and latched on as if that touch alone would bring him to orgasm. When I called him out on it, he claimed drunkenness to be the culprit, which I found convenient but not altogether improbable. He made himself at home with our wine and not that I'm keeping track, but we had two empty bottles at the end of the night and I only had two glasses myself. I wish I'd had more, maybe then I could've drank that evening into something interesting. But every time I looked over, Jacob seemed to be refilling his glass. Damien wasn't too far behind either, what with his low-key alcoholism. By the end of the night he was glassy-eyed and staring at me like a lecher at a strip club.

That was one of Damien's greatest flaws. There was always something pervy about him. He interpreted his actions as suave but really he behaved as if he'd been deprived of sexual contact for an eternity and would hump a tree if it gave him pleasure. It's the same problem most of the homos in this gay ghetto share. They intoxicate themselves to mask whatever self-loathing they constantly feel, then in their inebriation turn into scowling sex monsters.

That's why I hate going to the bars so much. The second I set foot in any of them, a room full of wasted men undress me and assault me with their eyes (sometimes with their hands as well, unfortunately). Why would anyone think I want their drugged out, sweaty hands all over me? I'll get a contact high just from their touch. And the fact that these homos state their drug use as "recreational" is hilarious. It's a habit at best, life necessity at worst.

At least now on the rare occasions that I do venture out I'm not the only brown person in the bar. This city's always been wildly segregated, don't get me wrong, what with the club night for black guys at Catch One and the Latin nights at Rage. But if you found yourself at Rage, you should've killed yourself already. It was so bleak.

That's part of the reason I believe Damien relished me so much. My skin color, that is. I could tell he thought me exotic and that my presence elevated his reputation in the eyes of others. We were an "integrated, diverse" couple, which in his mind made him a better person. It's not uncommon among the white men I've been with, especially the faux-liberals here in LA. They think having any person of color in their inner circle makes them an activist in BLM, and yet when their underachieving teenager gets waitlisted at their top universities they decry all the discrimination against white people. And don't dare tell them their child is underachieving. The lecture you'll receive will last longer than their college career. Yes, please tell me more about how much harder your son works than everyone else, when you all lived in Bora Bora for six months during his senior year.

As time dragged on our relationship felt so juvenile, as if I were shackled to my own teenage horndog masquerading as a man. I suggested I move out after a few months and that was not received well. I believe his exact cries were "does that mean you want to break up", "why would you leave me" and "don't you love me anymore". Mind you, I hadn't told him I loved him in the first place, but it didn't seem the appropriate time to highlight that.

I attempted to reassure him that this didn't mean we had to break up, it just might be nice to have our own space. He got wildly insecure and wallowed about how good it was living together. The whole fiasco became a three-hour episode. There were tears, there were shouts, there were hugs and kisses. We ended up having sex in the end and I dropped the idea of moving out. For the time being.

We continued on fairly uneventfully. He reestablished his fantasy bliss with me and he maintained some level of interest to me. It was mostly the physical that interested me, truth be told. His personal life was exceedingly dull. He had the maniac boss who in his mind he was always thwarting through mischievous antics, though I didn't trust how accurate his versions of the stories were. He reconnected with some old friend who'd wronged him, the lesbo who ditched him to move in with her lover. Part of me wondered if this whole game of playing house with me was an attempt at revenge on her, and the other part of me that might argue the contrary didn't care enough to do so.

Then one day I was at Trader Joe's picking up some almond milk and vegan butter when I literally ran into Mark. I always try not to make eye contact with anyone in public for fear of recognizing someone and being forced to interact with them when all I really want is to get away. So as I walked with my eyes on the floor, I physically rammed another person, who in my true luck of lucks turned out to be Mark.

He glanced at me with his sad brown eyes—I hate when people use the term "puppy dog" eyes, but he truly had them—and asked how I was. I told him I was fine and out of politeness asked how he was, and he unconvincingly told me he too was fine. I don't normally feel guilt as I believe it's a wasted emotion, but a small part of me felt it in that moment. He looked so somber but also like he started going to the gym. The long sleeve t-shirt he wore rolled up pulled at the biceps and chest in ways they never used to, and the veins in his forearms were more prominent than before. It appeared that he replaced his former fat-filled, forgettable body with a rather impressively muscular one.

As he talked, he longingly touched his hand to my arm in an attempt to establish a physical reconnection. He inched closer to me and it was obvious where his mind was going. So I decided to show him some benevolence and slept with him back at our old apartment. It was quite nice having that familiarity back, knowing all his pleasure points and him knowing mine. Damien was always naïve with that; he didn't know how to read a room.

But like most charity work, once the feeling of doing something good for Mark passed, a sense of dread washed over me. I realized I would have to tell Damien about my tryst with Mark and oh, what a scene that would be. It wasn't even the heartbreak and pain that daunted me, it was the amount of sheer time and energy it would consume that gave me anxiety.

The actual event was far worse than I could've imagined. If suggesting I move out brought down his world, this revelation imploded the entire universe. At one point I was actually concerned for his physical well-being, then at another I was concerned about my own due to whatever attack might befall me at his hands. I have some PTSD after Mark's surprise attack when I broke it off with him.

Damien's episode was a rollercoaster to say the least, and I strongly dislike rollercoasters. He called me names—"dirty slut", "cheating whore", "callous bitch"—and cursed at me like a sailor. I was so offput by his nasty language that I wasn't offended by the name-calling, I was offended by his vulgarity. It was a lot of "fuck you", "fuck him", "fuck this", everything fuck fuck fuck. I felt a bit of a prude to be honest. I never realized how much cursing put me off.

Then he wept about how much he loved me and what are we going to do and where do we go from here. I tried to console him but he threw himself on the floor—literally *threw* himself. I thought I heard him hit his head, and when he started flailing, feared that it might have caused a seizure. I'm still not entirely sure that didn't happen, at least for a moment.

When I tried to help him up was when he lashed out at me, thrusting his fists toward any part of my body they might reach. Thankfully my breakup with Mark improved my reflexes and I was able to dodge his attack before he made contact. Also I'm not sure you can even call what he was doing punching. Damien would make a terrible fighter.

Despite such a dramatic encounter, we persisted in our cohabitation. After he finally calmed down we went to our separate beds, but I later awoke to the sound of my door creaking open. He crawled into my bed and we had sex until dawn broke. There really is something uniquely special about post-breakdown sex. I don't know if there's a chemical discharge during the fits that elicits some primal urge, but those endorphins flooded our apartment that night.

The next morning he was making omelets and home fries. We were once again unified and I was not about to regress to the antics of the previous evening. Plus I was starving after hours of coitus. He was gleeful as ever, settling right back into his domestic bliss.

For such an ostensibly counter-cultural individual, he was surprisingly traditional. He clung desperately to that old fashioned nuclear family ideal, of which I had apparently become anchored in. Part of me wondered if one day he'd insist that I quit my job to stay home and rear the children. Were it not for his raging libido, I'd have expected him to stay abstinent until marriage.

We continued playing a "happy couple" for a few more weeks, when he brought over the former she-devil who was the first to destroy him—the lesbo roommate that is, not the psychotic boss. They'd each paid their penance and absolved each other over dinner some time before (at Café D'Etoile, I'm sure), and had been talking on and off since. Apparently this would be the first time she reentered the apartment since her infamous escape. Oh the excitement.

She arrived around eight pm with a dowdy spinster in tow who I learned was her live-in girlfriend. On the one hand, I was impressed by her devil-may-care attitude toward her appearance; on the other, you should have at least some pride in yourself. I truly believe her jeans had been left behind by a passing circus clown who decided to retire them after a solid decade of performances. And I'm by no means a professional hairstylist, but even I know about leave-in conditioner.

She proceeded to tell me that she was the manager of guest relations at the La Peer Hotel and I all but passed out from the shock. How in the world can a walking soup kitchen like that have a position at such a chic hotel? If I stayed there and she tried to relate anything to me, I'd request an immediate tetanus shot and the entire hotel be Febreze-ed round the clock. I don't know what nepotism got her that job, but she must have some good blackmail on someone.

We ordered in yet again, this time from Maggiano's. Apparently our house rule is to subject guests to the most vile meals we can come up with in the hopes that they never return. It must've held some sort of nostalgia for them, though, because the lesbos were ecstatic at the idea. They carried on about some incentive where if you ordered one pasta meal, you got a second for free, or something like that. And health officials say obesity is dying in America. We'll show them!

The lesbo former roommate shared Damien's affinity for movies, and they spent the evening speaking in tongues which someone explained to be movie quotes. The lesbo in need of a makeover tried to carry a conversation with me, but all I could focus on was the smell of rotten cheese exuding from her mouth due to the large portion of fettuccine alfredo she inhaled moments before. Luckily for her, that was one of the pastas under the buy one get one free deal, so she had another entire portion for tomorrow. She didn't seem very interested in Damien, or was trying to keep her distance. Or maybe she was trying to hoard all the fettuccine to herself. Who could tell?

I don't know how long the night went on, because it feels like it's still going. They began talking about that actress Damien loved again, and in my extreme boredom I think I managed to spiritually exit my body, and my poor remains will forever be trapped in that night. It was truly endless.

When it finally did come to a close, the two lesbos staggered out in a slightly drunken stupor. Damien was tipsy as well, as per usual. I chided him for his drinking on a variety of occasions but he never paid me much mind on that. We said our goodbyes, the ladies left and we capped off the night with a little romp in the bedroom.

One benefit to a drunken Damien is his loose lips, and I don't mean that as some sexual euphemism. He will blabber on about anything and everything. If you ever want to discover his darkest truths or someone's secrets, throw a couple drinks down his throat and wait.

That night he divulged to me the awkward encounter he endured when young Jacob met the wayward lesbians. It wasn't long after Damien first reconciled with his former roommate and he thought introducing his past to his present would bring his "inner circle" closer together. Well apparently, instead of coming together, these two worlds full on collided. Lesbo former roommate all but peed around Damien to mark her territory, ensnaring every conversation between just the two of them and excluding both her lover and Damien's newfound friend. Jacob, being the ever graceful and sophisticated person he is, merely sat and glared at them from across the room the entire time. I'm sure he was so filled with jealousy, he was greener than that animated ogre my nieces and nephews love to watch.

It's fairly obvious that the two of them did not like each other. From how Damien described it, it seems "despise" is a more accurate term for how they felt for one another. It sounds like the stereotypical *Will & Grace* complex, with Jacob trying to force his way in between Damien and B.

Social etiquette is not something that runs strong amongst these people. Upon meeting me, each of them asked about my Indian heritage. I know the education system in America is broken but geography can't be that hard. I'm from Sri Lanka, which is an entirely different country, though when I said that to any of them, I was greeted with a confused stare like I'd started speaking another language entirely.

That same stupid stare also extended to the pronunciation of my name. I've grown so weary of correcting people when they say it wrong that normally I let it go, but I kept hearing my mother's strong will insisting "CORRECT THEM EVERY TIME", so I did. The wayward lesbians apologized and moved on quickly, but simple Jacob spent almost thirty minutes trying to get it right. That's one thing I definitely won't miss about Damien, his orbit of extremely awful company. Not counting me, of course.

I was getting accustomed to our domestic situation when, out of nowhere, Damien told me that he bought a house. He'd escalated the situation with his deranged boss Eileen, who he whined about constantly from the moment I met him. To be honest she sounded unpleasant to be around at worst, but I really think he was just irritated that she seemed not to like him. The worst thing in the world for him is to be disliked. He's so overcome with insecurities that he instantly turns on anyone who doesn't like him in the hopes of expunging them.

But all I could think when he'd rattle on about her is why on earth would she ever like him? He'd always sing "Come on Eileen" when address-ing her because in his stupidity he thought it was funny, which shows how juvenile he is. Apparently he whined to the right people though, and they awarded him a large settlement for his supposed troubles. Once again the white male prevails.

This new purchase led me to believe that we'd all receive an upgrade so I was pleased, but he rudely informed me that it would only be for him and Stanley Kowalski. Needless to say I was taken aback. After our many cycles of romantic dependency, now he was going to rebuff me? I tried to hide my distaste but I must admit I don't have much of a poker face. Also, it was clear he was seeking some kind of recompense for what he perceived to be poor treatment earlier in our relationship. I wouldn't give him the satisfaction of thinking that I felt betrayed by this.

So at the end of the month he moved into his little shack in Laurel Can-yon. He tried to convince people he was living in the Hollywood Hills but that is far beyond an exaggeration. This was basically in The Valley, which is where the wayward gays who couldn't make it in West Hollywood go to wallow.

The Hollywood Hills, on the other hand, are elite and glamorous and very exclusive. I know firsthand, because I've actually been there. One of my ex-boyfriends Kevin was a personal trainer who worked with David Bo-reanaz, and if Damien weren't such an insanely jealous person, he would've loved that anecdote due to David's role on *Buffy*.

David had a party once and my ex brought me as his date. I'm very good at parties like that, everyone naturally thinks I'm an actor because of my looks. Damien amusingly told me he moved out here to try his hand at acting, to which I inadvertently laughed in his face. It was not intentional I promise, it's just so ridiculous to think of him on any screen that my natural reaction was to laugh. I couldn't even stop it if I'd wanted. But I guess every movie or show needs that sad loner for the audience to pity, so maybe Damien could nab one of those roles. I've never had much of an interest in the industry myself, but if I ever wanted to make a parlay into that world, it's nice to know the doors will be open.

When I told Damien the story of my ex, he fluctuated between elation at being two degrees away from his beloved Sarah Michelle Gellar, and infuriation at the acknowledgment of a previous relationship. He's such a child. He wouldn't stop berating me with questions about my ex. He probably thought we were still in contact and meeting in secret behind his back. Which reminds me, I should give Kevin a call.

But in comparison to that gorgeous compound I reveled in years ago, where Damien moved to was a hippy commune that smelled like patchouli and marijuana. The only celebrities housed in that area are aged poets and musicians who are still looking for a modicum of success. And the actual house he moved into would never be classified as anything near chic or glamorous. At best, it looks like a forgotten relic from someone's past that they remember fondly but upon seeking out later in life they realize how run down it's become. At worst, it's the shack an old witch would use to bake small children in her oven. You couldn't pay me enough money to set foot in there. I'd probably succumb to malaria or typhoid fever in that tragedy of a neighborhood.

Despite his tactless treatment of me at the end, what happened to him is still unfortunate. Honestly I think there's a strong possibility he did it to himself. As I mentioned, he was obsessed with that Sarah Michelle Gellar actress, and someone told me his passing was similar to one of her death scenes in a movie. He was not above doing something like that just to feel close to her. When he thought he offended her over the internet, he was part mortified that he might have hurt her feelings, and part exuberant that he might actually be interacting with her. It's an awful thing to consider, but definitely a possibility with someone as unstable as he was. I use unstable here as a kind euphemism for pathetic.

Or, speaking of unstable, it could've been Jacob out of jealousy. I hate to point fingers but we all know how those lost souls can behave. They're bitter about their misanthropic existence and lash out at those closest to them. He always seemed envious of our relationship so his pent-up aggression at not being able to have me could've finally erupted. It's sad to think that I could drive someone to commit such a dastardly deed, but a person that desperate will always try to latch on to someone who excels much more than they do. I can't be held responsible for how pathetic he is.

Thankfully I don't dwell in the past so I was able to move on pretty quickly. In my coping I resorted back to my old Grindr hookups and some new affairs at the gym. It's never my favorite having to be so common, but I'm not going to limit myself by being stubborn. Damien wasn't that spectacular of a relationship and the men in LA will always be drawn to me. I just have to find the right one for me.

THE SARAH MICHELLE GELLAR

Is this some kind of joke? Are you honestly insinuating that I might have something to do with a man's murder because a few people think it resembles "my" death scene in *Scream 2*? There are more plot holes in that theory than the *Scooby Doo* movies, and at least I got paid well for those.

Let's start with the most obvious—well, they're all pretty obvious but this is just the first one—I've never had a death scene because I'm clearly not dead. I've played characters who've died, many over the span of my lengthy and celebrated career, but personally I, Sarah Michelle Gellar, have never died.

There were a few close calls on a couple of sets, due to some negligent crew members who'll remain nameless, but as you can see I survived those (against all odds) to sit here writing this. Whatever this ridiculousness is.

Secondly, and equally obvious and important, I've never even met this person. I barely even know his name. Danny? Dominic? Whatever it is, I have zero connection to him, less than zero probably, so I'd have no idea how to find him to kill him.

Riddle me that, genius detectives. How does someone murder a person when they don't know who or where they are? Is there even a detective on this case? Have we defunded the police and I missed it? What is happening here?

I don't mean to sound so flippant, but you get what I'm saying about this, right? I'm sure he was a nice enough guy and this is a tragedy, so I feel for those who are left hurting.

Or maybe I shouldn't assume that. Maybe he wasn't a good person and no one's mourning him and he had this coming, I don't know. THAT'S the point. I have no idea about literally any details surrounding this person so in what world would I have gone through the effort of murdering him?

And someone mentioned some real loose story about an internet feud he had with me. C'mon, really? I can't believe I actually have to speak to this, and yet. For the record, THAT'S NOT A THING.

I have social media, sure, but you know what I don't use it for? Stupid internet feuds with people I don't know. Does anyone use it for that? It really feels like people are grasping at straws here, I'm sorry if I'm calling someone out right now but come on.

And you know what I especially don't use social media for? To internet-stalk myself. Again, who actually does that? I feel pretty safe in saying that no actual celebrity would ever be that desperate. We get enough shit (excuse my language) thrown at us, none of us would actively seek it out. And especially not to the lengths of creating a fake account to disguise ourselves.

Maybe one of those D-list influencers on the rise would do that—I don't even know their names. But we all know they're desperate for attention so would do something crazy like that. Have you checked if this guy had any influencer connections? If he did, pop them up to the top of your list, they'll do anything. Just don't expect them to be talented.

The most absurd part of this—well, again it's all absurd so I guess I should say yet another absurd part to this—is that apparently our supposed "feud" was because he said that I'd become irrelevant. I'm sorry, have you seen the success that is *Wolf Pack* on Paramount+? That show's basically breaking records, I toured the world promoting it and was celebrated with an award at the Cannes festival. CANNES, people. They don't give awards to just anybody.

Not to mention *Buffy*'s still on TV practically everywhere and I get fans reaching out to me almost every day telling me how impactful it still is for them. And those are just two of my TV shows. I won't even get into my film career. I still have fans coming up to me all the time quoting Kathryn Merteuil.

If this guy were a true fan of mine, why would he even go there? Real fans don't try to bring down their favorite celebrity by calling them irrelevant. I've got the millions of followers to prove that.

Also, if you knew me, you'd know I'm a perfectionist when it comes to details. You said he was just thrown through a glass door then over the balcony right? Well I know not "just", that's still pretty bad and painful and all. But if you've seen *Scream 2*, you'd know that my character was stabbed twice in the back before getting thrown over the ledge, so if I were going to recreate that I would've gotten all those details in. He wasn't stabbed at all, right? That's not a completed Sarah Michelle Gellar checklist, and you don't want to mess with my checklists. Ask Freddie and my two kids how often that happens.

Now that's leading me on a weird tangent, but this is already weird for me so I don't really care. But if I were going to murder someone based on one of my character's deaths, why would I choose one of the most secondary characters I've ever played? Granted, *Scream* is a huge franchise, but Cici was only in two scenes.

Do you know how many times I've played a leading character who died? I'd most definitely base a murder off one of my leading roles. Wouldn't any actor? I know everyone says, "there are no small parts, only small actors", but I'm pretty sure even Meryl would go for a major role like *Sophie's Choice* or *The Devil Wears Prada* over *Lemony Snicket*.

Even Helen Shivers would be better for me than Cici. That scene's at least universally considered iconic, despite it still being more of a sup-porting role. What, you don't believe me? Google it, there are tons of people who still talk about that chase scene. Plus my feet are still bruised from all the rocks I put in my heels to slow me down (I was in much better shape than my character was supposed to be). Which is why I, Sarah Michelle Gellar, didn't have a death scene—Helen Shiv-ers did. Note the difference?

But getting back to this guy who was supposedly such a big fan of mine, which—ok I know I just said I was coming back to him, but I have to say something. And there's no way of doing it delicately, so I just have to jump right in. I love my fans, I really do—my real fans, that is. I wouldn't have the success I'm blessed with without them. But what's with all these gay guys becoming obsessed with me?

I mean I love them, fans are fans and I would never discriminate, plus I love gay guys. They're super fun. But it's weird right? They're into other guys but idolize this beautiful woman they see in movies and on TV. Maybe because Buffy was such a strong, independent character who was a bit of an outsider they could relate to her? Or wanted to be her? I don't know.

And what's with this "mother" term? I'd never heard it before and neither had my gay friend Jeff until our press conference for *Wolf Pack* on Plus, but apparently that's what they all call me now. Or refer to me as? I'm not really sure.

I understand the "yas queen" and "yes mama" as exclamations and affirmations, but this seems more like a title they've given me. It's hilarious and an honor (I think?), and I love it as a sign of community love, but they know I'm not their actual mother, right? I guess I shouldn't assume that.

And does that mean they all have bad relationships with their real mothers? Are they looking to me to be a surrogate? That's really sad if that's the case. And I mean that genuinely, not sad like a pathetic loser in school kind of sad, but sad like I'm sorry you've had to live like that.

Or is it more of an Oedipal thing, where they weirdly want to have sex with their mom but that's too creepy so they identify me as a mother figure to fantasize about? That's still very creepy and if that's the case I'm really not ok with that.

So I'm officially uncomfortable now and frankly over this whole fiasco, so let me summarize: I, Sarah Michelle Gellar, did not know this man, never heard of this man before being brought into this sideshow, and I most definitely did not murder him.

If anyone needs to discuss further you're welcome to get in touch with my attorney, otherwise please don't contact me again. Also how did you get my contact in the first place? I need to double check our security. WHY AM I EVEN WRITING THIS???

THE NEW BEST FRIEND

Don't believe a word that bitch tells you. I know all he did was talk shit about me. He's a pathological liar, literally every word coming out of his mouth is untrue. From the moment I met him I knew he was playing Damien. He was dating another guy when they met!! 🙎 How were they ever going to have a good relationship when it started out like that?? I mean whatever I'd never call it a relationship anyway, he's a living sex doll and they had ZERO things in common so I'd say that's way more of a fuck buddy and probably even just a trick.

Ugh I can't stand him, I'm sorry. Every time I talk about him I flip out, I can't help it. He's seriously the worst. Like he always talks like he's hot shit and super fancy, and I'm like you're from Bakersfield and went to Cal State Northridge. FUCK. OFF. I'm from Wisconsin, I get it, I don't judge anyone because of where they come from but if you're going to be that big of a bitch and are from BAKERSFIELD I'm going to judge the shit out of you. Their biggest exports are STDs and meth, so which category do you fall under? Also you troll Grindr like it's your job because you don't have an actual job you're an "influencer" but not a good one (um eight thousand followers is NOTHING to brag about), and you're secretly working at a Jamba Juice in Topanga so none of the queens in WeHo find out.

God I hate him. 😈 I really hope he killed Damien. I mean, obvi I'm sad that Damien died and I wish he hadn't, but since he did I just hope we can find justice in punishing an asshole like Shrenik.

The first time I met Shrenik was at Damien's place. When Damien told me they were moving in together I raised an eyebrow both literally and figuratively. 😶 They'd been hooking up for a little while and at that point he sounded harmless, but still that's a weird step to take. He said they weren't serious and it wouldn't be a thing, it was mostly convenient for both of them. Shrenik was just coming out of a bad breakup (which he caused) and Damien needed a roommate since B hightailed it out of there with her girlfriend and his savings were drying up.

I mean, I would've thought Damien would ask me to move in with him cause duh, that's the obvious choice. But for whatever reason he didn't and I didn't want to bring it up cause I didn't really care. But seriously we would've had so much fun, and he would've never gone down the shit spiral that is Shrenik. But whatever, I tried to be optimistic and supportive, cause at that point I was like what's the worst that could happen? They have sex a lot for a while, get bored of each other and realize they have nothing in common and live out their separate lives until one of them decided to move out. Not so bad.

Well doesn't the universe like to kick me in the nuts. Shrenik is SO that bad and way worse. He's like a maniacal jellyfish—you don't know you're stung until he's gone away, but then he swims back and stings you again just to be sure you know you got stung. He's SUCH a dick. Like Damien told me one time they were at the Grove and this like five or six year old was running around them, kind of obnoxious but whatever he's a kid, and Shrenik stuck his foot out to trip him. And then laughed!! 🎧 Who would do that to a CHILD?? If I were that kid's parent I would've flipped out on him. I actually don't remember what the parent did, now that I think about it.

And god help you if you mispronounce his name. The first time I did he literally folded his arms like my mom used to when I was in trouble and gave me the cuntiest look, and was like, "It's pronounced 'Shre-nick'." He said it real slow like I'm some idiot. I'm sorry but it's not the most common name so calm the fuck down. My bad for making a mistake *once*. Asshole. OH! And then there was the time he gloated about having sex with that stupid Aaron Schock! I don't remember how he came up, we were probably talking about all the shitty people we see around town cause there are A LOT of them, and Shrenik's like, "Ohmygod I totally had sex with him, he's so hot." And I was like, "Um excuse me? He's a horrible person who tried to use his status as a senator to strip gays of all our fundamental rights and then took advantage of his own white privilege by hooking up with a guy at Coachella in public." And he was just like, "Whatever, he's hot. And the only reason people go to Coachella is to do drugs and hookup." Like that makes it ok!! He's so superficial, ahhh I hate him so much. And then he was like "And he's a *former* senator, he's not even in office anymore." Oh I'm sorry, are you trying to correct me now you stupid asshole?! 😒 come for me. (Hey Kim Chi!!)

I don't know why I was surprised though. He'd bend over for anything with a six-pack and a bank account. And that's the other thing, he'll never admit he's a bottom. Like it's so shameful. Um, maybe be a little more ashamed of your asshole attitude than your actual asshole. But don't get me started on bottom-shaming, I can't with all those masc-for-masc wannabe gym rats who are all "SUP BRAH I'M NOT SOME PUSSY MAN UP LOOK HOW MUCH I CAN BENCH PRESS", then get to the bedroom and lock their ankles behind their head squealing like a greased pig escaping a butcher. 😒 You suck dick just like the rest of us—if I'm a fag you're a fag.

So I get to Damien's and Shrenik's there and on first impression I thought maybe Damien didn't make that bad a choice. Shrenik is definitely hot in that WeHo way—he's got the permanent five o'clock shadow perfectly trimmed on his square-set jaw, the sides of his hair razored and perfectly faded up with long perfect hair on top that you know he spends so much time blow drying. And he's at the gym all the time so is super fit, oh and his skin is perfect with no pores and so insanely soft it's crazy. This one time I accidentally grabbed his arm and it was like holding a watermelon in a silk pillowcase. His skin was buttery smooth but the muscle underneath was so firm. I didn't know that was possible.

But whatever, no matter how pretty he is, he's still a dick and an asshole. Ha his two favorite things. Who am I kidding, they're two of my favorite things too, and every other homo on the planet. But he's like one of those guys on Instagram who in his bio is like, "I'm a PHD Scientist, Cancer Research Specialist and total nerd wah" but every photo is in a speedo in some different location showing off his eight-pack. Now I'm no medical researcher, but I'd think you'd have to stay in one location long enough to do whatever research you're bragging about being such a genius at. I mean, what exactly are you researching in a boy bikini poolside in Fire Island right after you were tanning at the beach in Mykonos in between raging it at every circuit party around the planet? Besides the mating habits of gays from around the world.

I know I sound cunty but I'm really not. If he'd been a nice guy I'd totally be down with him, and probably just be pissed that he's hot and nice and how unfair that is. But now I can be pissed that he's a hot asshole (which I'm sure is how he sells himself on Grindr). The first thing he said to me when I walked in the door was, "Have we had sex?" 💀 Uhhhh NO. How is that the first thing you ask someone you just met?? Is that somehow a dig or can you really not keep track? And when I said no I don't think so he was like, "Yeah you're probably right" and looked me up and down. Like he's judging me now! You just asked if we'd ever had sex like you legit don't know all of your sexual partners, and you're going to get judgy on me??

And THEN he started making fun of me for driving a Smart car and working at the Trevor Project!! A Smart car is the most environmentally friendly car out there (and don't give me that shit about Teslas, they're only doing it for rich people and Elon Musk's a fame-hungry asshole, so they can suck it), so excuse me for being concerned about the future of our planet. And who are you to make fun of the Trevor Project??? I'm LITERALLY saving lives and all you can do is Facetune your selfies so you look even more like a plastic doll. Way to make an impact. F.U.C.K.I.N.G.B.I.T.C.H.

So whatever, we're sitting around talking waiting for our food and Shrenik's in the chair across from us doing these like weird stretches and flexes, like showing off his muscles or something. At first I was like is he just really uncomfortable? I've sat in that chair before and never thought it was that bad, but maybe he had a really hard workout or something. But then he kept eyeing me while he was doing it and I realized he was showing off. Like I'd just start drooling all over just because he has biceps that can bulge on command. If you're trying to stretch sore muscles you don't imitate a dumbbell curl to flex your bicep or angle your arm so it perfectly displays your tricep bulge. It's like we get it, you've got a hot body. Put it away.

I doubt he was trying to hit on me cause Princess Cunty wouldn't deign to stoop to my level. He made it abundantly clear that he thought very little of me when he made quips like, "wow cargo pants, I didn't realize we were back in 1997" and "you could probably be pretty hot if you worked out like once or twice a week". FYI cargo pants have never gone out of style and I do the elliptical twice a week, thank you very much. I have bad knees so can only do low impact exercises. And yes Damien already made the "there goes your social life" joke when I told him about my bad knees, along with anyone else who's ever seen *Clueless*.

In an attempt to avoid any further conversation with the literal poser I suggested we watch *Sucker Punch*. I knew Damien loved it and I needed a little senseless violence at that moment. To my surprise, Shrenik was super into the movie too.

"Oh my god I love that movie, I've seen it like five times."

At this point I was still pretending to play nice so in an Oscar-worthy performance I held back my initial colorfully rude comments.

"Really? It doesn't seem on brand for you."

"It's the one where they're in a girls home and they have to fight their way out right?"

Ugggggggh she's so dumb.

"I mean, that's missing a lot of pieces and over-simplifying, but more or less. Sure."

I don't know why it surprised me so much. I guess I couldn't picture him watching anything more than like porns and stuff. 📽️

And on top of everything, that bitch completely bogarded the wine the entire night. He literally sat with the bottle cradled in his arm like Paris and her stupid chihuahua. He basically put a straw in the bottle and sucked the whole thing down. He's such a lush and not in the fun way, his is an intervention kind of way. If he even has any real friends who care enough to throw him an intervention—I'm sure as shit not gonna intervene for him.

The next day Damien called me to recap the night, as we always do after a night out (or night in, in this case). I was still lying in bed, not super hungover cause we know who hogged all the wine the night before. But not like Kimmy-Schmidt-excited to start the day.

"So last night was fun."

"Yeah." Another Oscar-worthy vocal performance.

"Shrenik's cool right?"

I paused but caught myself before it went on too long. "Sure."

"He's really funny."

I think I literally scratched my head when he said that. "Is he?"

"Yeah. What, you don't like him?"

"No, I didn't really get to know him well last night." Lie. I knew all I needed to know. She sucks.

Damien was dickmatized by him so it was kind of whatever. I couldn't talk shit about him while they were together but at least now I got why he was into him. If Shrenik wanted to have sex with me all the time I'd probably be able to put up with him more. I wish I could say I'm a bigger person than that but I'm not. I'd fuck him, just with tape over his mouth maybe.

But whatever, enough about Shrenik. I've wasted enough of my life talking about that bitch. Damien and I met in the bathroom of Mickey's, the dance club with after-hours that mysteriously "burnt down" and came back totally renovated thanks to the insurance money (🫥), so that pretty much set the stage for our friendship. It was after midnight, maybe around one so we were both a little drunk. We were at the sink washing our hands (hygiene, people!) when I heard the faint beat of a familiar song. I perked up to listen and saw that he had done the same.

"Is that—"

"Work Bitch!"

Like the stereotypical gays that we are, we both ran straight to the dance floor. We sang along to every vocal fry Britney forced out while shaking our asses. I don't pretend to be a good dancer but goddamn I'll bust it out when I hear one of my jams. Damien's actually a pretty good dancer, he always looks really good on a dance floor. Although it's typically pretty dark and I'm usually pretty drunk, so take that with a grain of salt. At one point I thought I saw him laugh at something across the bar.

"What are you laughing at?"

I was surprised he even heard me over the blaring music.

"I'm not laughing, I'm dancing."

He said it with complete glee and all I could do was laugh in response. They faded Britney into a song that I didn't know and if Damien knew it he wasn't interested either. We both stopped dancing and stood there. It was one of those awkward moments where we didn't know each other at all but just shared a weirdly intimate moment, and neither of us knew what to say.

"My roommate just moved out without telling me and now I'm fucked with the rent."

I didn't know what to say and didn't want to ruin my buzz so just came back with, "That sucks. Want another drink?"

He thought a moment. It probably wasn't the response he expected but I think he liked it. "Yeah." I bought him this round and we kept drinking the rest of the night.

When the bar closed, I decided to walk him home. I wasn't trying to get on him—I honestly wasn't interested in him like that. People always think there's something more between us because we're really close but it's never been like that. You know how you connect really intense with someone on a totally non-sexual level? That was our friendship. He's really more like a brother. So I totally wasn't trying to go home with him in the sex sense. He was just pretty drunk, and when I'm drunk I always think I'm more sober than I actually am so felt like I should take care of him. I was trying to guide him down the sidewalk and he started fumbling with his pants as he walked.

"Shit I gotta pee."

He unzipped and literally walked inside of a bush, like that Homer Simpson meme. I heard a rumble and a thud and some giggling. I should've known I was drunk cause instead of checking to see if he was ok I stood there laughing. He finally reemerged fighting the branches off of him and buttoning his fly.

"I fell in the bush." 😵 He was laughing when he said this.

"I heard." I was laughing when I responded.

"I think I peed on myself. Is it bad?" 😃

It looked like his dick became a sprinkler system that tried to water his body. There was urine all down his pants, on his shirt and sleeves and his face looked a little damp, but I couldn't tell if that was sweat or pee.

"Nah you're good."

We became friends pretty much instantly. Our shared sense of inappropriate humor really connected us. He hadn't met Shrenik yet so we were going out as single boys on the regular. One night we'd hit up Chapel, the bar that took over once Here closed (RIP Here, I loved that place!!), to pose with all the angular cheekbones and pay for overpriced cocktails until they side-eyed our obnoxious laughter, then make our way down to Gold Coast to end the night with cheap drinks and the friendly old queens who've been around since Stonewall. Gold Coast was my favorite dive bar, and not just because one night I inexplicably hit three bullseyes in a row playing darts *very* drunk. Apparently my athleticism kicks in when I'm about seven drinks in. But it was SO sad when they had to close, I almost cried when I heard the news. I seriously can't even believe it. Is there nothing sacred in this town??? 😭 RIP Gold Coast I miss you SO much!!

Other nights we'd traipse to Fubar for Big Fat Dick, get drunk and tip the gogo boys who were all sorts of nasty. There literally is nothing sacred in this town, because Fubar closed down too!!! Seriously what's a gay supposed to do in this town to hookup??? All the new bars are WAY too well-lit and forced to serve reheated frozen food but still charge like $20 a plate. Ummm if I wanted to eat Totino's Pizza Rolls I'd just microwave them myself, thank you very much. Also which of these bitches in WeHo do you think would eat at a bar anyway?! They want their ass blown out by a hot guy, not some leftover pizza bagels.

But I can't tell you any of our Fubar stories for fear of self-incrimination, but let's just say one involved a cherry and one gogo boy's surprisingly tight asshole. 😈 The actual craziest story from Fubar is the Sunday afternoon they had a screening of a football game. I guess the owner is from like Cleveland or something so he loved watching their football team play (sorry I don't even know who they are, sports *wheeeeeeeee)*, and showed the game in the bar when they played. When I first heard of it I thought it'd be cute, figuring it'd be all the local WeHo boys who like to pretend they're into sports but are really just in it for the tiny outfits that show off their legs (cause they never skip leg day! 💪). I'm sorry, joining the local kickball league does not make you a qualifying Olympian. I'm not being a bitch, I'm just saying.

So I skip on over to Fubar on a Sunday afternoon expecting a handful of cute gay wannabe athletes but what do I actually find? The ENTIRE bar filled with folding chairs occupied by the straightest of straights, men and women, screaming at the television and literally chest bumping each other by the bar. 😨 It was like I stumbled into an episode of the gay *Twilight Zone.* All I could do was stand in the doorway with my mouth gaping (go on with your slutty jokes). Did these people know less than twelve hours ago the extreme gay shit that was going on in that very room? Did they realize how much semen they were probably sitting in?? I've never been so stunned in my life, honestly. A talking giraffe wearing heels and a beret would be less surprising.

Damien was obvi my first phone call after that insane Fubar adventure, and we cleansed my palate of all that hetero energy by hitting up all the gay bars on the strip. I'm pretty sure that was the time I tried to sniff the gogo dancer's armpit at Mickey's but he refused and then wouldn't let me tip him anymore and Damien cursed him out for me, but I was a little toasted so that could've been one of our other outings. That's what our friendship was, a multitude of misadventures where we could always count on the other to ride along.

We have the same tastes too, we love a good trashy dive bar but every now and again like to pretend we're one of the elite. ☕ If we wanted to feel fancy we'd sit at the bar at Norah and have martinis, but Norah's so pretentious that I can only stand to be there for one drink so we'd end up back at Gold Coast again (still crying 💀). Occasionally one of us would find what we believed to be an attractive guy to make out with, and sometimes even go home with. Those were always pretty hit or miss.

"I can't believe you let me go home with that creature," he told me one time.

I think we were having brunch at WeHo Bistro this time. It's a tiny place off Holloway that everyone's been past a thousand times but most people never really pay attention to. The food was surprisingly good, and they have bottomless mimosas so naturally that's the real draw.

I sipped (fine, chugged) my mimosa before responding, "You kept saying how hot he was, I thought maybe I had reverse beer goggles." 💀

He matched my chug with his own. We were always tit for tat.

"Reverse beer goggles are not a thing."

"They totally are. It's when you're super drunk and think someone's hideous but they turn out to be pretty hot once you're sober."

"I got where you were going with it, I'm saying it's not real. He was a fucking creature."

I'm pretty sure I was eating French toast, cause I love French toast and always order it at brunch. So I'm pretty sure I was diving into that when I asked, "Was the sex good at least?"

Damien was more of a savory brunch person so I'm pretty sure he was cutting into some eggs benedict or something like that. "Of course not, he was gross."

Though I love me my food, I would NEVER talk with my mouth full.

Momma raised me right, so I'm sure I said this with fork in hand. "Sometimes the ugly ones can be eager."

"I had to run out. He asked if I wanted his number and I told him it was already in my phone."

"Classic."

"Next time you let me go home with someone like that I'm giving him your number."

"You already give guys my number."

I know we seem cunty but we sound a lot worse than we actually are. All friends talk about their tricks like that. The first time he hooked up with Shrenik was no different. He'd put himself on a self-imposed hookup diet and Shrenik was his cheat day. He didn't know it was literal cheating at the time.

"I totally made up for that creature last time," he gloated.

We were starting one of our epic nights on the boulevard, walking to probably Gym Bar. It's where the Sporty Spices like to pretend they watch sports but really just get drunk and grope each other. And while they too closed, at least they reopened again a little further down.

"That's not saying much."

"But like really made up. This guy was like porn star hot."

"Austin Wolf porn star or Ron Jeremy?"

"Total Austin Wolf."

"Ugh I love him so much. 😋 I'd climb that mountain of muscle in a heartbeat." But like really. I wish I could've found him during his escort days. I would've paid literally all of anyone else's money I could find to have him for a night.

"Bitch you wouldn't climb a thing. He'd have to go spelunking in that cave you call a butthole."

"Rude!"

"Oh please. It's like throwing a hot dog down a hallway."

"Um excuse me, to be that loose you'd have to get laid more than once a lunar cycle, which currently I cannot claim."

"Not now, but in the height of your ho-dom...and that shit's permanent."

"Fair. I'm assuming the sex was good then?"

"Oh yeah. It was like fucking a Ken doll. He's all pecs and abs and muscles. And he'll do anything."

"Ah, childhood trauma?"

"Probably. Desperately Seeking Susan's Approval."

"That tracks."

I didn't know it at the time but Shrenik's need for validation would later validate my idea that he's not as great as he wants everyone to think. He's so full of shit. Not that I want anyone to have childhood trauma, obvi that's terrible. But he probably has some and totally deserves it.

Shrenik latched his claws into Damien pretty quick. They hooked up three or four times that first week and Damien claimed they had a real "connection". 🙄 The only connection they had was dick to hole, cause that's the only way Shrenik knows how to connect to a person.

Damien was going through a lot so I think he was pretty literally fucking the pain away. He was really stressed about suddenly living alone, and his job was getting crazier than usual. It was a day job for him to begin with, since he moved out here to be an actor. He had a really shit time when he was really pursuing it, the assholes who run "the industry" can be so nasty.

He told me about *numerous* casting agents he'd meet who'd literally laugh him in the face and tell him he didn't have "the right look". I'm sorry, but from a purely objective standpoint Damien has all the right looks so I don't know what they're talking about. And I've never seen him officially act in anything, but he showed me these short films he made in college and he's really good! Some of them are a little artistic, like there's one where he's like a Beeker-inspired science assistant who always wears an old World War II era helmet and gets pelted with an egg from a window or something, but even when I didn't get what was going on he was still really funny! Honestly he's one of the funniest people I know, I'm always peeing laughing when I'm with him. So he definitely could've been on a sitcom or something like that. It sounds like all those "industry" types are all a bunch of misera-ble bitter assholes who purposefully set out to destroy another person's dream.

So on top of him not really wanting that job, he had to deal with his psycho boss Eileen too. I call a lot of people psycho when they cross me or someone I'm close to, but I think she was actually mentally unhinged. He called me one time cause she told him she was going to "fuck his face off", can you believe that??? 😂 All I could do was laugh.

"What does that even mean?"

He was laughing too. "I don't know but she meant it."

"Come on Eileen." I sang it like the song, I know it's probably lame but it makes me laugh every time. Damien loved it too. "Did you report her to HR?"

"Oh I've got a list going. I'm getting that bitch fired."

"Why does she hate you so much?"

"Who knows. She's a miserable person, she hates everyone."

If she didn't hate him before she definitely did after he got her fired. 😐 She FLIPPED out apparently and went after Damien before security dragged her out of the building. Like literally dragged, she was kicking the air and screaming and everything. She managed to get her hands on Da-mien before they got her out and was slapping him and screaming about how she was going to ruin him. I'm sure she included more expletives than Damien recounted, she sounded like the type who didn't shy away from a crop-dusting of f-bombs. Damien thought about pressing charges but the company offered him a nice settlement and corner office, so he backed down. And that settlement allowed him to buy his big fancy house, so it all worked out. Well, except for his former boss. But she cray anyway.

In between the psychotic tendencies of his boss and those of Shrenik, Damien reconnected with his old friend B. I still haven't been able to get her full name from anyone, somehow every time I bring it up a wild tangent ensues. I'm guessing it's something lame like Bridget or Basic. She's the type who would never let herself go by anything she deemed common. She was the one who moved out of the apartment and ushered in the era of the Satanic Ken doll, but I feel like there's a backstory I'm not privy to. He never really talked about her when I first met him, then out of the blue he was just like, "I texted my old friend B the other day."

We were at his place watching one of the movies we've watched a thousand times together, probably *Best Little Whorehouse in Texas* or something else with Dolly. And drinking, duh. 🤓

"Who's B?"

"My old roommate, the one who moved out."

"Oh that's cool. Are you guys talking again?"

"Starting to. We'll see."

He's super not good at talking about his feelings so I learned whenever he clammed up it was something important. In that moment he was clammed up so tight I think he made a pearl.

"Do you feel good about that?" I tried to tread delicately, but I'm also a big sharer.

"Yeah I guess. I've missed her." For Damien to admit that he missed someone is HUGE. He's like the king of playing it cool 😎 So I knew this thing with B was a big moment for him.

Damien and her first reconnected over a dinner out cause I think they both wanted neutral territory, and the next time they got together he invited me over. She was coming back to the scene of the abandonment crime for the first time since it happened and bringing her girlfriend, so I think Damien wanted reinforcements. Psycho bitch Ken doll hadn't moved in yet so I donned the camo (not literally, camo's not really my jam).

I went straight over after work and as always was the first one there. Even before Damien. He's notoriously late, which I should've known, so I sat on the doorstep for about twenty minutes before he got there. 😑

"Why'd you get here so early?" He was still halfway down the driveway when he shouted.

"I told you I was coming right from work." I didn't get up until he was standing right in front of me. He didn't have any real sense of urgency.

"Oh yeah." He was never terribly upset about being late. Just one of those things he didn't concern himself with. He opened the door and tossed his leather man bag on the floor beside the entryway. "You want something to drink?"

"Nah I'll wait till they get here. Don't want to be wasted right when they arrive. Do you need help setting up?"

"Setting up what? It's just B, we're not entertaining the royal family."

"What would you set up with if you were entertaining the royal family?"

"Probably the good champagne."

"You have champagne?"

"No. But I'd get some." He grabbed himself a Peach Bellini Smirnoff Ice from the kitchen.

"Bitch beer?"

"Don't judge. I'm revisiting my roots."

"So are you going to smoke clove cigarettes and sleep next to the toilet after you puke?"

"There's a strong possibility. Sure you don't want one?"

"Fine."

I'm highly influenced by those I'm close with. Plus those Smirnoffs taste like candy.

When B and her girlfriend arrived we were each on our second Smirnoff and sat on the couch. She rang the doorbell and Damien just stared at the door, almost confused.

"Just come in." He sounded offended that she'd expect him to open it for her.

"I just wanted to be polite," she said as she entered.

"Since when?"

"Save the attitude till we've at least sat down, ok?" she said with a slight jest in her voice, but she also meant it.

Not gonna lie, on first impression I was a little intimidated by B. And not cause she's a black woman!! I didn't mean it like that, I don't subscribe to that angry black woman trope. I love me a strong black woman, Angela Bassett and Viola Davis are total goddesses, and Lizzo's my motherfucking jam. Play that flute while you twerk that beautiful booty gurl!! She's totally representing for us big girls. And I don't care about any of that lawsuit drama, I still love her. Cause that's all it is, D-R-A-M-A!!

But B's like really tall, and I'm not just saying that cause I'm short. She's at least six foot so she def has a presence. And she's one of those cool look-ing people who just kinda owns the room. Does that make sense? I don't know. I guess it's the nerdy high schooler in me who still gets intimated by the cool kids. And her girlfriend Lily had a cool look too. They look like a lesbian power couple for sure. Lily's definitely more of the fem but not like full lipstick lesbian. She has more of a 90s throwback kinda style, which is totally my vibe. I bet she knows every cool vintage store in the city, and probably any other city she's been to. I never get how people always know how to find the good ones, I feel totally left out. Anytime I walk into a thrift store I'm like oh cool, another Billabong shirt from my childhood. Thanks.

We made pleasantries for a while—and by while I mean the first few drinks—with Damien behaving as if we were all long time friends needing no introductions. He was never really good at inter-personal relations. He knew what he had with everyone around him but either wasn't interested in or didn't understand how everyone else interacted.

But B and Lily seemed nice enough. Damien and B had a very brother-sister relationship, antagonistic but mostly playful. Lily seemed to be used to it, or at least succumbed to putting up with it. She was quiet for most of the night so I didn't get to know her very well. She didn't seem particularly interested in being there.

At one point B looked around the apartment and quipped, "You haven't done much with the place."

"I didn't get much of a heads up so haven't figured out my design scheme yet."

"Your design scheme is usually naked men and Ikea."

"Well we can't all shop at Home Depot or they'd have nothing left in stock."

Lily just sat and rolled her eyes at their digs, occasionally giggling at one of B's. I couldn't tell how much they were trying to slash at each other. It felt like a knife fight but with plastic sporks so no one really got hurt. At times it felt like Damien and B were the only ones in the room, and Lily and I were behind some two way mirror. We were literally on the outs with them too. Damien and B sat next to each other on the couch, and Lily and me were relegated to the chairs watching them. No one really engaged with me that much and I wasn't too keen on inserting myself into their "playful" pestering of each other.

I drank that night comfortable so by the end I was pretty tipsy. They'd put on some movie Damien and B used to watch all the time—*Lone Star State of Mind,* I have no idea so don't ask me about it. Josh Jackson was in it so that was some nice eye candy, but in my drunkenness I didn't pay attention to much else in it. Damien and B laughed together through the whole movie, and Lily looked even more pissed about being there so didn't say much to anyone. I left before anyone else cause I was turning sleepy drunk and was, frankly, fairly bored. No one seemed to notice though, Damien just gave me a farewell grunt and Lily looked at me like a prisoner watching a fellow inmate escape. B didn't even acknowledge it.

We hung out a couple more times after that, nothing particularly exceptional. B never bothered to feign interest but was civil enough with me. For whatever reason I don't think she likes me that much, but it's so fine cause honestly she's not my favorite either. She's not super friendly like at all, and she's so serious all the time. Like have a laugh once in a while. And Lily always seemed strangely non-present. I couldn't tell if she didn't remember me, didn't care or just never wanted to be there. I think it's a combination of the first and third, or maybe all three actually. Damien never paid her much mind and never really talked about her, so I get the feeling they're not all that close either.

Not long after my first intro to them was when Damien dropped the bomb about his fuck-boy moving in. We were at Tramp Stamp Granny's for their drag show on Monday night—per Damien, "Monday's are the new Thursday, Thursday's the new Friday and if you're out on Friday and Saturday night you should just kill yourself."

I should've known then that something was amiss. Before Shrenik moved in Damien and I were at the bars every weekend, having the best time laughing and dancing and drinking A LOT, so this sudden shift to conservatism had to be Shrenik. He probably wanted Damien home all the time so he wouldn't realize how many better guys are out there. Like any guy is better. Fucking bitch.

It was between drag numbers and Damien out of nowhere shouts, "So I finally got a roommate."

"Sweet, is he hot? Can I sleep with him and never call him and make it super awkward?"

"He's definitely hot, but you can't sleep with him."

"Boo why not?"

"Cause I already am."

"Wait what? You're moving in with a trick?"

"Not moving in like that. He's not poking holes in the condoms trying to get pregnant. He'll be in B's old room, so we'll just be roommates."

"Uh ok. Sounds real weird."

"It'll be fine."

"Which one's moving in?"

"Remember Ken doll?" He saw my eyes go wide. "Yep, him."

"Thank god. If you said it was one of the ugly tricks I'd have slapped you." Oh to be so naïve again.

"Nah this'll be good for everyone. I'll get money for rent and sex whenever I want it."

"You're such a smart little hooker."

"Everyone who comes to Hollywood's got a dream."

"If he's your Richard Gere then that makes me your Laura San Giacomo, so you have to get me something nice."

"Kit doesn't get anything nice in the end."

"Vivian had to get her something after all Kit did for her, they just didn't show it."

"That's a stretch."

"Cause the rest of the movie is so realistic. I'm sure there are many hookers on the streets of LA who've gotten swept off their feet at the Regent Beverly Wilshire and gone on to live happy successful lives with their new rich husbands."

"All I heard was bitch."

"Bitch, you heard me."

"You're like Charlie Brown's parents but cunty."

That was generally how we talked to each other. We weren't being nasty, just joking like all friends do. It wasn't as bad as it sounds. 😕

So Shrenik moves in and it all goes to shit. I really only heard from Damien when there were problems. They were usually about Shrenik, but even when they weren't he still called me. Shrenik can't handle real situations so when Damien needed an actual human being and not a sex doll I was the obvious choice. His presence had strained our friendship, but the worst part is I don't even think Damien noticed.

The first time he called me in tears was two weeks after the apartment dinner date. I refused to be the first to call so we hadn't spoken at all. On the sixth day I was furious, I couldn't believe he hadn't at least sent a text. I swore that when he finally did call he'd get a tongue lashing like he's never had before. By the eighth day I was a little depressed. Did our friendship mean that little to him that he could just forget about me and lose all contact? Or was Shrenik really trying to isolate him all to himself so Damien wouldn't get any ideas about leaving him? That thought sent me into savior mode. 🙇 If Shrenik was really trying to trap him, maybe I should step in to rescue him. Maybe Shrenik's even more of a psycho than I thought and he had Damien holed up with no means to escape. I'd really spiraled down this whole *Misery*-type plot when I finally got his call.

"Girl where have you been?" I saw his name on the caller ID so didn't bother with formalities.

Even before he spoke I could tell he was in shambles. I don't know maybe it was intuition, but I swear there was something in his breathing.

"Shrenik and I got in a huge fight."

I'm not gonna lie, I let out a huge sigh of relief when I heard that. If Shrenik was the extent of his problems this was going to be better than I expected.

"Aw I'm sorry, what happened?" You still have to pretend to feel bad.

"He got really mad at me cause he said I'm not committed enough to our relationship."

"What relationship? I thought you guys were roommates who had sex occasionally. Or more than occasionally."

"I mean yeah, but it's kinda becoming more than that."

"So this was his plan all along."

"No it's not like that. It just...happened."

"How does he want you to be more committed?"

"That's just it, I don't know! It's not like I'm dating other people."

"And you're already living together. Jesus, are you getting married?"

"No of course not, I barely know him."

"Well you're living with him and not dating other people, so what else is there?"

"I don't know. I just..." He got quiet and all I could think was oh god, please don't say it. But he did. "I think I love him." 😨

Then it just slipped out, like a knee-jerk reaction. "Ugh why?" I immediately regretted it.

"What? You don't like him?"

This was one of those precarious situations. I didn't want to lie to my best friend, but I def couldn't be honest either. What's he going to say when I tell him Shrenik's a mego-maniacal vain self-obsessed idiotic pathologically lying loser who's only positive attribute is the perfect body he works so hard to keep and thinks VERY highly of? "Oh cool thanks, I never really noticed that before. You really opened my eyes, you're such a good friend." *Sex and the City* didn't even play it that dumb. (But I love you *SATC*! Everyone tells me I'm Carrie 😊 And we're gonna pretend *And Just Like That* never happened.)

"No he's fine, it just seems like this is more than just a coincidence. Like he's been thinking about this from the beginning."

"Even if he was thinking this when he moved in, is it that bad that he wants to be in a relationship with me?"

"Of course not. It's just a little manipulative. And maybe that's not the case, I just want to bring up other angles that you might not be seeing since you're so close to the situation." I patted myself on the back for that one.

"Yeah."

"And listen, if I'm wrong I'm wrong. I hope I am." I wasn't. "Cause if that's true then he's not someone you should trust." He's not.

"No you're right. I don't think that's the case with him, but I get it. You're watching out for me."

"Always. I got yo' back."

"I know, I love you for that."

"I love you too. Just make sure whatever you do is at your own pace. Don't get pressured into anything." Damn, I was on a roll.

"I will. I gotta go though, he's coming back inside."

I hung up thinking I'd effectively laid the seeds to be rid of Shrenik for good, but the next day Damien told me they had the best make up sex he'd ever had. That fucker was good. They had a few more spats that all went down the same—Damien crying cause Shrenik was upset about some made up shit he wanted Damien to feel guilty about. Then they'd have sex and all would be right in the world.

The second time I thought I was making progress in the anti-Shrenik movement, but after that I realized Damien wasn't leaning into it the way I'd hoped. So I pretty much adopted the same script from there on out— "I'm sure he didn't mean it that way", "Make sure you're protecting yourself", etc etc. 😬

We were going through kind of a rough patch in our friendship. Damien became this crazy insecure shell of himself, we didn't hang out nearly as often and when we did ALL he talked about was his weight. He started drinking protein shakes and going to the gym like a maniac. He was probably going like three times a week or something. I know it doesn't sound like a lot but before Shrenik the only exercise he got was raging all night on the dance floor.

And he never wanted to leave his house. I tried so many times to get him to come out and he was always like, "I'm tired sorry" or "Shrenik wants to just hang and watch TV sorry". He was never really that sorry cause he was staying in to have sex with Shrenik all the time. I told you, he had him dickmatized.

Finally I got sick of never seeing my friend and guilted him into going out. I called him in a kinda bitchy mood, but I think I'd earned that.

"Are you friend breaking up with me?"

"Of course not, what're you talking about?"

I was happy he answered, but also a little bummed at how surprised I was that he did.

"I haven't seen you in weeks."

"I've just been really busy."

"Yeah, with your live-in sex toy."

"Work's been crazy too. They're finalizing the case against Eileen so I've had a ton of meetings."

"Well that's all good but I still want to see you."

"Ok so how about lunch this weekend?"

"Lunch? Why don't we go out one night?"

"I don't know, I'm so over the WeHo scene. Everyone's so basic."

"So? We always had fun laughing at the basic bitches."

"Let's just do lunch and go from there."

"Ok whatever."

Lunch was almost worse than not seeing each other. Lunch is where you take a work meeting that you've canceled on three times already and are forced to see. And to make it worse he insisted that we go to Tender Greens cause he had to get a salad.

"Since when are you eating salads?"

We were scooting our trays down the cafeteria-inspired checkout. I get that it's going for casual, and a lot of places are doing that now, but when did it become ok for such overpriced places to have such an antiquated layout? I mean I'm no interior designer but really guys? Put a little more effort in at least. Especially if you're gonna charge me $20 for a sad falafel wrap.

"I really want to lose ten pounds."

"Ok Regina. Are you using foot cream as face lotion too?"

"My face smells like peppermint."

We'd paid and made our way to a table by now.

"Why do you want to lose ten pounds? You look fine."

"I've got this gut, I look pregnant all the time."

"No you don't."

"I've been going to the gym more, can you tell from my arms?" He flexed, and if he weren't my best friend I would've laughed.

"You know if you put on muscle you'll gain weight."

"Whatever, you know what I mean."

"Let me guess, Shrenik's been saying you should work out more."

"No, I just go to the gym with him. I like going to the gym, I just needed a workout buddy."

"And I need a drinking buddy."

"You should be careful, you've been drinking a lot lately."

"Bitch don't even start with that shit. You drink way more than I do."

"I know, I was drinking way too much. I've been cutting back. It's helped a lot with my gut. You should think about that too." His eyes slowly descended to my waistline beneath the table.

Rudeness aside, this was beyond our normal friendly bickering. There wasn't even a hint of sarcasm in his tone.

"Hold up, no. What is happening to you?"

"Nothing, I'm just trying to be healthier. It's not a bad thing."

"Fine be healthy. Obviously that's a good thing. But don't come for me because I'm not the perfect WeHo size."

"I'm not coming for you, I'm just saying you should think about taking care of yourself."

"And you should think about talking like yourself. This isn't you. This is all the shit we've hated about everyone else."

"Hate's a strong word. I'm trying not to be so negative."

It was like I was sitting with a Stepford Gay. This was not Damien talking, he was regurgitating some bullshit ideas someone had pushed upon him. And that someone was that stupid bitch Shrenik.

He always thought he was some health god who could look down on all the sad fatties beneath him. Damien never cared about anyone's weight, especially not mine. When we first met I was a little insecure about it—ok REALLY insecure about it, especially in WeHo—and he was the one who told me, "Fuck all these bitches. Literally. Go find the hottest one here, take him home and fuck the shit out of him." And I did. Any bar we went to I'd scope out the hottest wannabe Abercrombie model, start flirting with him and sure as shit I'd get him to come home with me. Cause I'm FUCKING AWESOME. Fuck whatever all those skinny WeHo bitches say.

And I'm so sick of hearing "every body's beautiful". My body is fucking beautiful and I don't need you to tell me. It's always the aging twinks saying that when they're crying about how fat they feel after a night of drinking. *"Ohmygod my cheeks are so puffy, I'm sick of people fat shaming me every body's beautiful wah."* And then they'll be the first to side-eye me when I'm walking on to the dance floor. Fuck all y'all, especially Shrenik. I want to just punch him in his stupid six-pack.

But then the winds of change started blowing. It all began when Damien got his big settlement at work. He called me super excited for the first time in a long while. Even though we weren't talking the same way we used to, we both pretended like nothing'd changed.

"They're basically giving me the rest of her salary for the year in addition to a raise and a promotion."

"That's awesome, now you're officially a sugar daddy."

"I'm not old enough to be a sugar daddy."

I laughed. "You're old enough to be a sugar granddaddy. So what're you gonna do with all that money?"

"I think I'm gonna buy a house. I hate living in apartments."

"Good call, sugar daddies don't live in apartments."

"They also can't be under the age of forty."

"I've seen the AARP catalogs you get. Where are you gonna look for houses?"

"Probably the hills. I like it up there."

"Sugar daddies live in the hills so that works. I bet Shrenik's excited." I was totally phishing but whatever.

"I haven't told him yet." 🎧

Had I been wearing pearls I would've clutched them. My heart was all aflutter as I let out a silent exhale of glee. "Are you going to?"

"I don't think so."

I held my breath in one of the biggest moments of anticipation of my life. "Why not?"

"I don't know. I don't think I want him moving with me."

🐵 I literally shed a tear right then and had to bite my tongue not to sing out in blissful harmony. The bitch's reign was finally coming to an end. This was going to be more satisfying than watching Cersei getting publicly humiliated and imprisoned.

"But don't say anything. I don't want him finding out until I tell him."

"Of course! I'd never say anything."

If I didn't care about my friend so much I totally would've found Shrenik right then so I could rub his stupid face in it. But I never talked to him (like he would deign to converse with me even if I wanted, stuck up bitch) so it didn't matter anyway, I just really wanted to be there when Damien told him so I could see him cry.

"Why don't you want him moving with you though?"

"A lot of reasons I guess. You know all the fights we've had. And he slept with his ex."

My mouth dropped in shock at this. I wasn't surprised that Shrenik slept with his ex, he's totally the person who'd do that. Hello, he slept with Damien while they were still dating! What I couldn't believe was that Damien never told me until now.

"What? When?"

"A little while ago."

"Why didn't you tell me?"

"I don't know. I know you don't like him and you would've told me to get rid of him." True. "I wanted to figure out how I felt first."

I can't say that didn't hurt, but I got it. I've never been good at hiding my feelings, and my feelings against Shrenik were strong (obvi). I wasn't going to try to make Damien feel bad for excluding me from something so important in his life, I'm not a manipulative psycho like Shrenik. So I let it go. But then Damien dropped the real bomb.

"And he hit me one time."

Now, I'm normally pretty good at controlling my emotions around people but when those words crept through the phone into my ear

I.

L

O

S

T.

M

Y.

S

H

I

T.

Big time. So much so that I couldn't even wrap my brain around it.

"Hold on. What?"

"It was a while ago. We'd gotten into another fight and he hit me."

"Are you kidding me? That bitch hit you?" I felt safe in letting my true feelings out.

"Yeah."

"Where?"

"In the face. I had a little black eye for a bit."

"Are you serious? He hit you IN THE FACE?"

"It wasn't that bad."

"He fucking hit you! It's always that bad!"

"I'm fine. Seriously."

"I'm gonna kill him. I'm going to find him and actually murder him."

"Please let this go. This is why I didn't want to tell you."

It did hurt to discover that my best friend hid something from me yet again. Especially something as monumental as this.

"Yeah why didn't you tell me?"

"Because I didn't want you flipping out, and I knew you would."

"I'm allowed to flip out! This is a flip out moment."

"I don't want to make a big deal about it. It's done, I've moved on."

I was glad that he moved on but I hadn't. I mean there was nothing for me to do but I really wanted to do something bad to that psychotic manne-quin. How could someone be so awful?!?! I mean I know he's hot but can't he at least *try* to be somewhat of a good person??? I seriously don't under-stand how anyone could like him outside of wanting to have sex with him.

Like he has this group of like really smart, really successful and really hot friends! They call themselves the Brown Boys Club, I met them once when Damien invited me out with him cause he was intimidated to meet them all. We met them at Pump, they were all sitting at a table in the back of their outdoor patio section under the trees like they were holding court. And after seeing them I don't blame him. They're all seriously REALLY hot, I don't know what they put in the water in South Asia or wherever these guys are from but they're all insanely good looking. They all have beautiful perfect hair, really thick and silky looking (why is mine starting to thin already??? I'm too young for this), perfect smiles with bright white teeth, and are all really fit (one of them was training for the marathon, ugh why?!). And super successful too, like one of them owns his own event planning business and does all these high profile weddings and big corporate events, and travels all over the world. And another is a big wig at Netflix, I think he's the VP of marketing or something super important like that. AND they're super nice! The rest of them actually asked me questions about myself, and actually listened when I answered and were interested in what I had to say! (or at least pretended to be, and were good at pretending.) But then they let stupid Shrenik tag along?! I get that he checks the super hot box, but the only thing she's successful at is sucking a big d. And we know she's not nice so they can't think she fits in with them there either. He must've manipulated his way into that group the same way he did with Damien, cause they can't be that interested in him as a person.

But whatever, they're not my business, I'm just so glad Damien was able to see through Shrenik, even if he did keep him around longer than he should've. And if any of those other Brown Boys Club members want to go out for a date or even a hookup, caaaaaaaaaall me!! I'm way better than Shrenik, promise. 😊

Damien eventually found a really great house in the hills and had an easy time with escrow. He was set to move in pretty quick so when he told Shrenik it was like a blunt force trauma—swift and painful. And now it was Shrenik's turn to lose his shit. He refused to leave, refused to pack any of his belongings and basically refused to acknowledge that any of this was actually happening. I wish I could've been there to watch his tantrums, I would've told that bitch off so hard. But I didn't want Damien to think I was taking pleasure in this, even though I totally was. But he didn't need to know. During his whole move he kept telling me how he couldn't believe he'd been sleeping with Shrenik for so long and how could he have even been around him so much. He finally saw his true colors, and not in the cute Cyndi Lauper way.

I helped Damien move into the house and it was beautiful. It's so peaceful up there, it feels like you're in a sanctuary. You can actually hear birds chirping during the day and crickets at night, instead of car horns and drunken shouting. It makes you feel like you're not in the city, which I learned I'm super into. There's a lot I love about LA but the parts I hate about it are really tearing at me. Like the layout of the streets makes absolutely no sense! Gardner just suddenly becomes Vista once you go below Santa Monica??? There are so many streets like that, it makes literally no sense. Whoever was the city planner had to be on some serious drugs. San Vicente!! San Vicente dead ends at Sunset in WeHo then magically reappears in Brentwood. Figure out some new street names people! It can't be that hard. Domingo Ave. Calcutta Blvd. Mango Road. See?

But whatever. That's why I love Damien's new place, it's so removed from all the LA bullshit. It has these gorgeous views of the mountains and all these trees. Greenery, the outdoors! And all of his neighbors kept telling him about the coyotes up there and to be careful if he had a dog. He seemed a little freaked out but thankfully Stanley Kowalski's an indoor cat so it wasn't much of a threat. Honestly I was kinda hoping we'd see a coyote at some point, I've never seen one.

Also, and I know this is going to sound really terrible and super cunty, but a little part of me hoped that Stanley Kowalski would get eaten by a coyote. I know, SO awful, but that cat is evil. 💀 I love animals, like LOVE, and fully donate to rescue shelters because every animal should have a home. But Stanley Kowalski is legit some spawn of the devil dogs or devil cats or whatever hell hounds protect Satan. EVERY time I was over Damien's that stupid cat would sit right at my feet and stare me straight in the eyes. And not some cute "oh will you be my friend" kind of stare. It was an "I'm gonna fuck you up bitch" kind of stare.

I swear, no matter how drunk I got, I never stayed over at Damien's because that cat freaked me out. Maybe it's better Damien never asked me to move in with him. Stanley Kowalski one hundred percent would've murdered me in my sleep. And it was only me! He never did anything to stupid Shrenik, like way to misplace your hatred, cat. Know your enemies. If I ever go missing or wind up dead, definitely look into Stanley Kowalski. I know I sound insane and paranoid but I'm telling you that animal is not to be trusted.

But ANYWAY, we got Damien into the house and started hanging out like we used to. Not exactly the same, he was still pretty over the WeHo scene which I was fine with. After a certain point you end up seeing all the same people when you go out so much, so I'd pretty much run the course on any guys I was interested in (and those who were interested in me). We'd hang in his house and drink and watch movies and I would do my best to avoid Stanley Kowalski. It was fun, we were back to normal.

Then the week before he died a bunch of strange things happened. You know when you're in the middle of something and you can't believe how this sequence of events unfold, then when you're looking back you're like oh duh, I should've put that together and done something about it instead of just let it ride out. That was this week for me.

It started out on Tuesday night when Damien and I decided to test the waters at Conservatory, the new restaurant that opened up where Beach Nation used to be, which opened up where Irv's Burgers used to be and probably a dozen other failed restaurants before that. Quirky note: the tiny lemonade-stand type structure that apparently housed Irv's Burgers is for some reason a historical landmark in the city of West Hollywood. Apparently they give away that title pretty indiscriminately since the place looked like a dump. Probably the only thing historic about it was that thousands of queens douched in their bathroom before hooking up with randos down in Vaseline Alley (IYKYK).

So we go to Conservatory and naturally it's filled with all the A-gays and A-gay wannabes. Every new restaurant opening is like when a new twink moves to town, a gay Batsignal goes on and everyone swarms around to see how good he's going to be. Usually the guys are a disappointment, but I hoped Conservatory wouldn't be too.

Thankfully I was pleasantly surprised when we walked in. Whoever designed it gets a big pat on the back, it was like high-end nautical chic or something. We got a cute little table off to the side and as the maître d' sashayed us over in his cool leather jacket and heeled black boots we scanned the crowd. Between Damien and me we either knew or had slept with more than half the people in the restaurant. There were a lot of fake smiles and awkward avoidances as we sat down. 😶

And yet we persisted, ordered some wine with our lovely little chipmunk of a waiter and were scanning the menus when I hear a voice beside me say, "Of course you're here." I looked up to find B and her girlfriend standing in front of the table. B had her arms crossed over her chest and was glaring at Damien, and she was NOT happy. Lily stood behind looking super cool but also super annoyed by the pit stop.

Damien laid his menu down super casually. I don't think he caught B's death stare. "Oh. Hey B."

"Hey. Thanks for the invite."

"We just came to grab dinner real quick."

"Nice that you managed to come all the way down the hill for that."

"I came straight from work."

He hadn't, but it didn't seem like a good time to point that out.

"So who's feeding Stanley?"

"I'll feed him when I get home, he's fine."

"Hope he doesn't shit on your couch."

"He'll be fine. Thanks for the concern."

Lily took a not-so-subtle step toward their table so B started to follow. "Enjoy your evening."

We sat there for a minute after they left. Damien continued reading the menu and I stared at him, waiting for some kind of clarification on what just happened. When I realized I wasn't going to get one without pressing for it I spoke up.

"Uh, what was that?"

He glanced up at me as if I'd asked what my name was. "That was B."

"Yeah. Being super weird."

"She's always like that."

"Not really. At least not with you. Did you guys have a fight?"

"No."

He was so nonchalant I let it go, but for the rest of the night I kept catching B glaring at us from across the restaurant. I don't want to say hate, but there was total hate in her eyes. She was pissed about something.

We got a little sauced on wine so hung at our table longer than we probably should've, but near the end I noticed that B and Lily had left already. I was relieved actually, I thought they might come over again for another confrontation. Now we could drink in peace.

Until we got outside. We walked down the handicap ramp and there she was standing on the corner. Literally just waiting for us. Her girlfriend wasn't there so I'm assuming she didn't want to be a part of this scene, because B laid into Damien real good.

"WHAT THE FUCK?"

"Oh hey B."

"Don't fucking oh hey me. What the fuck are you doing?"

"Jacob and I just had dinner."

"I can see that, I'm not a fucking moron. You're a piece of shit."

Damien in his drunkenness just laughed. "You love me."

"I don't fucking love you, you don't love someone who treats you like you don't matter."

"Of course you matter, you're my favorite."

"Fuck off."

"You're the one who left me for your stupid girlfriend."

"YOU ditched ME for dinner with HIM. And I tried. I tried to fix us but..."

She was starting to back away, and she either couldn't think what to say or was too angry to actually say it. I think the latter cause like I said she was pee eye ess eee dee (Pised? Ha love you Selma! 🙃) PISSED.

"There's nothing to fix."

She stopped walking and stared Damien straight in the eyes after he said that.

I felt like a really weird third wheel standing there watching them both. I tried to hide but there was legit nothing for me to even stand behind, so I ended up awkwardly shuffling in place like a pre-teen at their first co-ed dance. Finally B just turned and walked away. Damien watched her for a second then continued walking down the street. I scampered behind him.

"So she's not pissed at you?"

"No, she's good."

And we didn't speak about it again.

I called him Thursday night to try to convince him to go out that weekend. Truth be told I'd hit a bit of a dry spell in the bedroom department and I really needed some male attention. My last relationship was going on three years ago 😫, and while I don't mind being single like at all I was starting to feel a little spinster-y. And I love me a night out, don't get me wrong, but the hardest part in LA these days is just figuring out where to meet people. Not to totally age myself, but when I first started dating my ex, Grindr didn't even exist so all we had were the bars. They were always loud and fun, and you could chat with everyone and make out with this guy or go home with that guy or both. Now it's like I see the same seven people every time I walk into any bar on Santa Monica. And not that I'm a huge whore but I've also exhausted all the possibilities in my Grindr radius, so what's a gay to do? Drink I guess.

At least Damien always made a great wingman, so I tried to recruit him for the mission.

"Hey what're you doing?"

"Just leaving Gelson's. I got that tiramisu and princess cake from the bakery department."

"Shame eating again?"

"Not even ashamed anymore."

"Wanna go out this weekend? It's been a while since we've seen a bar, I'm feeling nostalgic."

"I just told you I'm bringing two cakes home. What about that says I'm in the mood to be around judgy queens?"

"Ugh come on, I really need to get laid."

"Go on Grindr."

"I've worn out that resource. And you really need to get laid too."

"I'm not feeling that at all. Guess who I just ran into."

"John Stamos."

"No. Remember that guy Robbie I told you I kinda dated a while back."

"Not at all."

"Yes you do. The dumb one with the big dick."

"That doesn't really narrow it down. Well actually it does, everyone says they have a big dick, but most are lying."

"He definitely wasn't lying. Anyway I just ran into him and he looks really good."

"Did you buy the cakes already?"

"Yes."

"Did he see the cakes?"

"Yes."

"Brutal. Think he'll fuck you again at least?"

"Doubtful. The breakup wasn't so great, and he's definitely still got his revenge body."

"You fucked that one up."

"Sure did. So yeah, I'm not feeling up to being around the gays of WeHo."

"Fine, wallow in your self pity all weekend. I'll live text you updates."

And then the cherry on top happened Friday night. I went to Fubar (one of my last times, waaaaaaaaaaaaah 😭), and was on my third Absolut and soda with a splash of cran. I was trying to figure out if this cute guy in a buffalo plaid shirt was into the guy he was with (which, if he was, he shouldn't have been—the other guy walked past me and I almost drowned in his shitty cologne, it was disgusting. Cologne should be discovered, not announced—and that one should just be forgotten), when Damien texted me.

"Dude craziest thing"

He always machine-gun texted one phrase at a time, so I had to wait to hear what this crazy thing was.

"Just saw Shrenik"

👀 I didn't wait for him to continue and immediately texted, "DON'T FUCK HIM" and he wrote, "Is this bring out my exes week??"

He didn't respond to my warning so I don't know if he actually slept with him or not. In the moment I didn't pay attention to his non-response, and turned my focus back to figuring out if the guy standing next to the DJ booth was lumberjack Brawny hot or lumberjack white trash. Also not to go totally off topic but can we talk about how hot the new redesign of the Brawny man is?? That square-set, bristled jaw line and visibly muscular chest under the flannel shirt??? 🪓 You know they had some kween up in there saying they needed to modernize just so she could get her fantasy man on all their packaging. And that GAWD she did, I love it!!! I never cared about my paper towels before but I sure do now.

And that's weird that Damien had all those run-ins right before he died right? I mean it might be a coincidence, two of them probably were since only one person killed him. I told the police all this when they called me, I mean after I stopped crying. Cause I cried A LOT. Damien and I were so tight, he meant everything to me. I think I made the officer who called uncomfortable, he got all weird, like, "are you ok?" Ummm no I'm not ok, you just told me my best friend was murdered!! WHY would I be ok?!

But that probably means I was the last person to talk to Damien right? Well except for Shrenik since he probably did it. God I hope he gets locked up forever. I'd go visit him in prison just to see how often he gets the shit kicked out of him.

So yeah, I guess I should wrap this up. If anyone knows anything please come forward. And Damien, if you can read this wherever you are, I miss you SO much and love you and am so sorry this happened. (also I totally pulled at Fubar that night!! Lumberjack was new Brawny hot and a super good lay 😄).

I wish I could tell you all about it!! 👀

THE CAT

row-
wwwwwwwwwwwwwwwwwwwwwwwwwwwwwwwwwwwwwwwwww
wwwwwwwwwwwwwr

meow meow meow meow meow meow meow meow meow meow meow meow meow meow meow meow meow meow meow meow meow meow meow meow meow mwuah mwuah mwuah meow meow meow meow mwuah meow purr purr purr purrrrrrrrrrrrrrrrrrrr purr purr purr purr purr purr purr purr purr purr purr purr purr purr purr purr purr purr purr purr purr purr purr purr purr purr purr purr purr purr meow meow meow meow meow meow meow meow meow meow meow meow meow meow meow meow meow meow meow meow meow meow meow meow meow mwuah meow meow meow meow meow meow meow meow meow meow meow meow meow meow meow meow meow meow meow meow meow meow meow meow meow meow meow meow meow meow meow meow meow meow meow meow meow meow meow meow meow meow meow meow meow meow meow meow meow meow meow meow meow meow meow meow meow meow meow meow meow meow meow meow meow

slurp slurp slurp

purr purr purr purr purr purr purr purr purr purr purr purr purr purr purr purr purr purr purr purr purr purr purr purr purr purr purr purr purr purr purr purr

purr purr purr purr purr purr purr purr purr purr purr purr purr purr purr purr purr purr purr purr purr purr purr purr purrrrrrrrrrrr purr purr purr purr purr purr purr purr purr purr purr purr purr

mwuah mwuah mwuah mwuah mwuah mwuah mwuah mwuah mwuah mwuah mwuah mwuah mwuah roww roww roww roww roww roww roww roww roww roww roww roww roww

meow meow meow meow meow meow meow meow meow meow meow meow meow meow meow meow meow meow meow meow meow meow meow meow meow meow meow meow meow meow meow meow meow meow meow meow meow meow meow meow meow meow meow meow meow meow meow meow meow meow meow meow meow meow meow meow meow meow meow meow meow meow meow meow meow purr purrrrrrrrrrrr purr purr purr slurp smg slurp

mwuah mwuah mwuah mwuah mwuah mwuah mwuah mwuah mwuah mwuah mwuah mwuah mwuah mwuah mwuah mwuah mwuah mwuah purr purr purr purr purr purr purr purr purr purr purr purr purr purr purr purr purr purr purr purr purr purr purr purr purr purr purr purr purr purr purr purr purr purr purr purr purr purr purr purr purr purr purr purr purr purr purr purr purr purr purr

purr purr purr purr purr purr slurp slilyurp slurp slurp slurp roww roww roww roww roww roww roww roww roww roww roww roww roww roww roww roww roww roww roww roww roww roww roww roww roww roww roww roww roww roww roww roww roww roww roww roww roww roww roww roww roww roww roww roww roww roww roww roww roww roww roww mwuah mwuah mwuah mwuah mwuah mwuah meow meow meow meow meow meow meow meow meow meow meow meow meow meow meow meow meow meow meow meow meow meow meow

meow meow meow meow meow meow meow meow meow meow meow meow meow meow meow meow meow meow meow meow meow meow meow meow meow meow meow meow

purr purr purr purr purr purr purr purr purr purr purr purr purr purr purr purr purr purr purr purr purr purr purr purr purr purr purr purr purr purr purr purr purr purrrrrrrr mwuah mwuah mwuah mwuah mwuah mwuah mwuah mwuah mwuah mwuah mwuah mwuah mwuah mwuah mwuah mwuah mwuah mwuah mwuah roww roww roww roww roww roww roww roww mwuah mwuah mwuah mwuah mwuah mwuah mwuah mwuah mwuah

meow meow meow meow meow meow meow meow meow meow meow meow meow meow meow meow meow meow meow meow meow meow meow meow meow meow meow meow meow meow meow meow meow meow meow meow meow rowwr rowwr rowwr rowwr rowwr rowwr rowwr rowwr

rowwr rowwr rowwr rowwr rowwr rowwr rowwr rowwr rowwr rowwr rowwr rowwr rowwr mwuah hisssssssssssssssssssshrenikssssssssssssssssssssssssssssssssss

slurp slurp slurp slurp slurp slurp slurp slurp

THE MURDER
(from another perspective)

Of course I'm not going to tell you who I am. That would be ridiculous and I'm not a ridiculous person. But everyone sees people who commit an act like this as these unhinged dregs of society, and that's not what I'm about at all. Not that I need anyone's validation or am trying to justify my actions. It's complicated, and I think people need to be confronted with that. Plus going through something like this is not easy from this side either.

The whole drive up Laurel Canyon, I was sweating. Like first date sweating. I'd made up my mind to do this and I wasn't going to turn back, at least not yet. Those stupid canyon roads didn't help ease the stress. Every blind curve felt like a whip around Mr. Toad's Wild Ride, and the line of cars behind me made it well known that they thought I was driving too slow by honking incessantly. How fast can someone go on these roads without killing someone? And yes of course I hear it, but I wasn't trying to kill myself or a random stranger with my car.

And then I was parked in front of his house. You know when you're driving and you don't realize that you stop paying attention as your mind wanders to a thousand different topics, then you suddenly find yourself at your destination with no recollection of how you actually got there? That's what this was. I might've driven through someone's backyard, I might've even run someone over on the way. I know once again it's so ironic to say this since I was on my way to murder someone, but I would've felt really guilty if I'd hit somebody on the drive up there.

The house was dark so more than likely Damien wasn't home. He was probably on some Grindr hookup or something. That's all he ever thought about. At least this would make sneaking into his place a whole lot easier. I skulked up the walkway that stretched up the right side of the house to the back patio. It was pitch black and I didn't want to use the light on my phone in case his neighbors saw. Not that I think any of them ever talk, but I didn't want to test it out now by drawing their attention. I stumbled on one of the steps about three quarters of the way up, which of course created a noise that seemed to echo through the canyon so I froze. I stood there for a minute listening to hear if anyone noticed the scuffle. It was still silent.

The door at the gate of his patio squeaked as I pushed it open, but this time I didn't panic at the sound. The only sign of life from the other houses were the lights in the windows of the one three doors down. This is one of the few moments where it works in my favor that no one gets to know their neighbors in LA.

I tried the handle on the kitchen door but it refused. Of course he locked it. I didn't expect it to be that easy, but I kind of hoped it would be. There were still the sliding glass doors to his bedroom at the opposite end, I just needed to find a rock or something to throw through it. I scanned the patio for anything that might work. I never realized how much crap Damien collected, I don't think I ever noticed it in his apartment. Is that an alligator pool floaty? He doesn't even have a hot tub, let alone a pool. And the plastic folding chairs as patio furniture is so pathetic. Even if he's trying to be ironic, it just reads tragic.

Of course there was nothing that would be useful in breaking glass, and as I wandered past the sliding doors I wistfully tried the handle. To my great luck and surprise, he'd left that unlocked. It might just be that easy.

Quietly I slid the door open and stepped inside, careful to be just as quiet as I slid it shut. At this point I wasn't concerned about the neighbors, I was doing it more in case Damien happened to be home with no lights on. It was a little before eight pm, so there was no chance he'd be asleep, unless of course he was in some drug-induced stupor which I shouldn't have put past him. Not that I think he did drugs, I shouldn't start spreading rumors now. And I don't want to be a gossip, but he seemed to have a self-destructive streak.

I stepped into the room and audibly gasped when I saw a pair of eyes glaring at me from the bed. Thankfully it was just his stupid cat Stanley sitting in the middle of the bed, staring with judgment like he always does. He didn't meow or make a sound, he just watched me come in. As if this whole murder scheme wasn't stressful enough, I had to deal with a cat trying to unnerve me. I've never spent much time around cats but in the few times I interacted with this one, he felt especially deviant. He had no alliances, just a personal desire (and excellent talent) to intimidate everyone. I listened more to hear if there was movement from the rest of the house, and when there wasn't I surmised that Damien definitely wasn't home.

Since I had the house to myself I meandered about to figure out some plan of attack, and snickered that this is the first time I used that statement in a literal context. Of course I didn't turn any lights on, since who knew when Damien might return. Also I figured this would help when I actually pounced on him, since the odds are that I'd have a better chance if he couldn't see me coming. But I needed a weapon. I know, I should've come more prepared but like most of my rash decisions this one came to fruition pretty abruptly. Like when I got my first tattoo, it seemed like a really great idea to get VEGAS BABY in cursive while on a drunken trip to Reno with my high school clique. I was stuck answering, "But why didn't you get RENO BABY" anytime someone saw it and heard the story—because of course no one would ever get RENO BABY and we couldn't afford to go to Vegas at the time—until I finally gave up and had it removed. And of course there's not a single person currently in my life who knows that story, so don't bother asking anyone.

On the weapons front, his house didn't provide much help. He had a nice set of knives in the kitchen, but I pulled one out and it didn't feel like a good choice for me. At first I envisioned myself wielding it like Vivica A. Fox in *Kill Bill,* but I slashed at the air a few times and it seemed like he could find a way of defending himself against it. Or worse, get it away from me and try to stab me. At that thought I promptly replaced it. I shuffled toward the stairs to his living room while searching for other possibilities but found nothing. I cursed myself for not thinking this through more.

Suddenly the house shook and what sounded like an airplane engine revving up echoed around me. I thought it was some combo of an earthquake and bomb ignition but quickly realized it was his garage door opening. I panicked and ran back into his bedroom, where Stanley remained in the middle of the bed with his yellow stained eyes of judgment. He was probably laughing at how much I was fumbling this, and thinking how much better he could do. Which I have to say is probably accurate. If anyone were to plan a murder well, it would be Stanley. I snarled at him then reminded myself of the task at hand.

The entrance door to the house creaked open and I heard Damien step inside. Do I abandon this insane plot or go full throttle? The door to the patio was right there and I couldn't decide, looking back and forth between that door and the one from his bedroom that opened to the rest of the house. When I heard his footsteps ascending the stairs, I knew I had to choose so impulsively slid his closet door open and stepped inside. Thankfully Damien has a double closet with mirrored sliding doors on both sides that he always keeps closed (I think he was still scared that monsters might live in closets? Tonight wasn't going to help that fear, though the effect would be short lived. Pun very much intended, of course). It was roomy so I had plenty of space to stand, and I looked down to my left and hey, a bat. I gripped the handle, happy to find my weapon and thankful this kept getting easier.

Under the door I saw the light to his room go on.

"Oh hello Stanley Kowalski, how's your night so far?"

Of course he would address his cat like he would any human. It's so stupid that he always called him by his full name. Also pretentious. It's an animal, it doesn't have a full name on a birth certificate. It should be called something like Fluffy or, in his case, Satan. He always had this look in his eyes that creeped me out, like he was plotting something.

"That good huh? Mine was whatever, but thank you for asking."

He had full conversations with an animal that can't speak. He was even more pathetic than I thought.

He slid open the other door of the closet and I held my breath. It passed just millimeters in front of my nose. He tossed a pair of crusty yellow Converse on the floor and closed it. I slowly let the air out of my lungs as the door slid shut.

"Oh by the way I hate my life. Everyone sucks. Well except you of course. I'm ordering La Scala and watching *I Know What You Did Last Summer* to cheer up if you'd care to join. Don't judge."

Of course he'd order something over the top like La Scala. He always has to go for the most pretentious option so he could feel fancy. If he'd gone for something like Maggiano's I might want to get in on that. I could go for some pasta right now.

Damien was convinced that Stanley understood everything he said to him, and if that's true then Stanley must want to murder Damien more than me. He has to be so tired of these banal statements that Damien thinks are conversations. And if he really did understand Damien, then like everyone else on the planet he wasn't interested in watching a twenty year old horror movie that wasn't so great the first time around. He remained firmly planted on the comforter.

Damien left the room, turning the light off so I was back in the dark, and I heard him turn on the TV in the living room. If he was going to watch *I Know What You Did Last Summer* that gave me about an hour and twenty minutes, since he always stopped it right before Sarah Michelle Gellar dies (he didn't like watching her go through that, as if turning off the movie somehow changed the fate of her character). I hate that I know so much about this movie.

So now what was I going to do? Charging into the living room while he sat lazily in front of the television seemed clumsy and with a high risk of going awry. I didn't really want to stand in this closet for an hour and a half, but this bat felt like a sign that this is where I was meant to be.

Grudgingly I leaned against the wall and waited. All my murderous nerves quickly diluted to boredom. How am I supposed to wait to commit a murder? Patience is a virtue but it's a real buzz-kill in a situation like this. I cleared some space between whatever colored hi-top Converse I was trampling, since I couldn't differentiate between any of them in the dark. The hangers carrying all his flamboyantly patterned button downs kept stabbing at me so in a flash of annoyance I pushed them all toward the opposite end of the closet, not thinking about all the scraping noise it would make. I froze again and listened, but thankfully only heard the sounds of fake fireworks coming from his television. At least he'd started the movie.

I decided for my own benefit to pop a squat amongst the shoes. It would limit my interaction with stray hangers and prevent me from turning into a hunchback. Also I'm lazy and hate standing for long periods of time. I checked my watch. Eight thirteen. Crap, it was still so early. I bent my head back and let out a silent ugh. This was going to be painful. I closed my eyes in an attempt to center myself. If I let my mind wander to a negative place I could screw this up and get myself hurt, or even worse, caught. How would I explain to everyone a plan for attempted murder? I have no idea what the jail sentence would be, but a lifetime of judgment and guilt would be the punishment from everyone I know and that would be plenty.

The doorbell rang and my heart jumped again. I may have dozed off or just been in a boredom-induced trance, but I started to panic. Did he invite someone over? Was the trick he most likely hooked up with earlier coming back for seconds? That food reference began a train of thought that eventually brought me back to his earlier discussion with Stanley that he was going to order dinner, and I calmed down as I realized it was most likely the delivery person. I heard a brief mumbled discussion then the front door closing as the delivery person exited, which confirmed that thought. I checked my watch again, thinking that had to have been at least an hour. Eight forty seven. Seriously? Since when does anyone deliver that quickly in LA?

I had to find something to occupy my mind. Listening to *I Know What You Did Last Summer* from afar was never anything I'd wish upon myself, and I could really only hear the high-pitched screams and startling music anyway. Trying to figure out the patterns on his shirts using only the dim light from my Apple Watch entertained me for all of eight seconds. But it did let me know that I'd hit my second ring of exercise for the day, so that was a momentary win. I tried to check on Stanley by squinting through the crack between the wall and the sliding door but I couldn't get my left eye lined up right.

Finally I began evaluating my life and how I found myself here. Not just physically here in Damien's closet, but life as a whole. Waiting silently for a murderous plot to pan out surprisingly created a great moment of reflection. I have an excessive amount of pent-up aggression resulting from many years of torment from the small-minded hicks I grew up with. After I moved away, I always felt proud that I rose above and never engaged with them, letting them think they'd won but really I'd moved on to such a better life. But now I really just want to punch them all in the face. I don't care if I have a better life now, they were douchebags to me then and when those two boys told me in the third grade that I was too weird and no one would ever love me, I should've kicked them both in the balls. But I didn't of course, I smiled and pretended they didn't hurt me like my mom told me to. And now when someone cuts me off in traffic, I turn silently ballistic and want to go *Falling Down* on everyone.

That might be warranted actually, the traffic in LA is completely out of control. There is an excess of stupid people hiding out in Los Angeles, and apparently they all reveal themselves the moment they get behind a steering wheel. Everyone just cuts you off or changes lanes without looking or makes a sudden turn without a signal, and then will cuss you out for being in the way. And why are there so many people in LA all of a sudden? There are way too many cars on the road at all times of the day. Whoever keeps building all these condos on every corner needs to be shut down. I'm about to embark on a murderous rampage just to thin the herd.

This probably explains how I wound up physically here, gripping a base-ball bat and waiting to bash Damien over the head. Rationally I understand he hasn't done anything so terrible that I shouldn't be able to move on and just forget about him. But emotionally I need to take it out on him violently. I cannot let his dickery go unpunished, and his constant success in life is not providing him with any consequences. It's not just him either. This city is overrun with self-involved, entitled pricks who believe they deserve every-thing thrown at their feet. I've had to deal with these narcissists for way too long and I'm sick of it. Ergo I will be his consequence, which brings my life full circle to when my aunt sat my cousin next to me as a punishment one Christmas when I was fourteen. I was reading on the couch in the fam-ily room while the rest of my extended family was in the kitchen and living rooms gabbing when my aunt drags my seven-year-old cousin in by the arm. "Sit on the couch there and think about what you've done." My cousin scowled as she hunched over next to me. Apparently I was awful then and age hasn't improved me that much. So I'm really just fulfilling the prophecy.

My trip down memory lane stoked the fire in me again and I was ready to go. I didn't realize how hard I'd been grinding my grip on the bat, and I gave myself a little rug burn on my palms. I shook my hands out then froze, hearing footsteps. It sounded like Damien was coming toward the bed-room. I slid up the wall so I was back in standing position in case I needed to pounce. Then I heard the sound of the toilet seat raise and a surprisingly loud stream of pee. I noticed another door in the bedroom when I first came in but hadn't investigated enough to realize that there must be a bathroom off the bedroom too. Then the toilet flushed and he was on the move again. He didn't even wash his hands.

He came back into the room and Stanley must've still been in there, probably sitting staring at the closet. Too bad Damien couldn't read be-tween the lines.

"Ugh I ate way too much, I feel gross. Why do I always do that?"

I heard him flop on the bed, probably dramatically flailing his arms out, and he groaned.

"I'm so bloated. Next time don't let me order pasta again, no matter what I say." He waited a moment, then continued, "Will you get me some water please?" I imagine he was staring at Stanley for a response, which is so weird and sad. "You're not much help, Stanley Kowalski."

I began to wonder if something more serious was wrong with him. It can't be good to have a full on one-sided conversation with an animal right? A little talking I get, but I think he seriously thought they were engaging in a real talk. That's not normal.

The bed creaked at what I presume was him getting up. Maybe he shouldn't have had that pasta, it sounded like he did a number on the mattress. He shuffled out of the room again, presumably back to his precious SMG.

I perked my ears to get a better sense of where in the movie he was. At this point I decided my best plan of action was to get him when he went to sleep. That way he'd be totally off-guard and in a position that would make it hard to defend himself. But if I had to wait all night, that was going to be tough for me. Having not subjected myself to any SMG or scary movies in well over a decade, I couldn't figure out how far we'd made it. There wasn't any screaming so probably wasn't anyone's death slash chase scene. I thought I heard a man chuckle, but that could've been Damien quietly sobbing in a fit of self-pity and/or at the upcoming demise of his TV love.

I leaned against the wall and was resigning myself to a seemingly endless wait when I heard footsteps approaching again. This time it also sounded like lights were being turned off, and sure enough he came back into the room with a groan.

"I'm giving up, I don't care."

I heard him unzip his pants and prepared myself in case he opened the closet door again. He did not. I heard the soft slump of denim being tossed on the floor instead. I followed his footsteps to what I presume was the bathroom again and saw a faint light turn on in the distance. I listened to him brush his teeth, which I've never heard anyone spit so loudly. I've actually seen videos of camels spitting and they do it significantly quieter.

He's disgusting, but at least he's got decent dental hygiene. The distant light went off and he shuffled back to bed, groaning once again as he laid down. He was so melodramatic, no one was even in the room (that he knew about, of course) and he still had to play up his discomfort to get whatever imaginary people he thought watched over him to feel sorry for him. Anyone who felt sorry for him for any reason is a moron.

I held off a minute for him to hopefully fall asleep. As much as I wanted him dead I really didn't want to have any interaction with him. Listening to him beg for his life would be the worst. "No please, you can't do this to me. I'm so special and the world will miss me and how will everyone go on without me?" Barf. Or he'd probably ask to make sure he looked good first. He's so vain.

The sound of Stanley snoring was my signal that enough time had passed. That cat was so loud I couldn't tell if Damien was asleep too, but I figured if Stanley had enough time to pass out, then so did he. I started to slowly slide the closet door open when a huge creak came from the other room. I immediately stopped and my eyes went wide. It was audible enough that it must've woke Stanley up too because his snoring stopped. Shit, had Damien in fact brought someone over? There were no follow-up creaks so it didn't sound like someone walking around. Maybe it was just the house settling? It seemed like that would happen in houses up here. But I definitely heard it and so did he, because he got out of bed to investigate. It took him an excessive amount of time though, I do not understand what he was doing. It sounded like he was rolling on the floor? I tried to squint through the crack to see but only saw him stand up. I jumped back in surprise. Shit, was he going to come for the bat? I gripped the bat tighter but thankfully he didn't open the closet. I heard his feet pad out into the hallway instead.

I took this as my opportunity to make a move, also because I was starting to get dreary so I needed to get this over with so I could go to sleep. Trying to murder someone is an exhausting rollercoaster of emotions. I finished opening the closet door and stepped out. Stanley was spread out at the foot of the bed and perked his head up when he saw me. He didn't move at all beyond that, much to my benefit.

I crept quietly past him out into the hall, holding the bat tightly with both hands. Damien stood a foot or two before the top of the stairs. He was staring out at the view through the sliding glass doors in the living room, engrossed in whatever trivial thought process he has. I wonder if a person has any sixth-sense type awareness before they're attacked? If, on some cellular level, he had an inkling this was coming?

I didn't spend too much time pondering that as I had to figure out where to make my first strike. The head would be the obvious choice, but Damien's taller than me and the angle at which I had to hit him might be weird, so I was worried I might not get enough force behind it. He also probably has a thick skull that would soften the blow. I thought I remembered hearing somewhere that hitting someone in the lower back with enough force would pretty much disable them, so I decided to go with that.

He must've been in some kind of trance or something because I stepped within a foot of him and he never moved. I took my t-ball stance— legs spread shoulder width apart, knees bent and bat held above my right shoulder—and readied my swing. Damien had the perfect target in the cherry blossoms of his culturally appropriated kimono, which I couldn't figure out when he had time to put that on. I took aim, lifted my left leg and swung with everything I had.

The sound of the bat hitting his back is nothing like what you hear in movies. They make it sound like when you squeeze a head of old lettuce, but in reality it's more of a shattering sound, like if you threw a bag of ice on the ground to break it up into tiny pieces that'll actually fit inside a glass. Also it's been a long time since I've hit anything with a bat (and only baseballs or softballs of course, I'm not some bat-wielding maniac) so I forgot how the impact reverberates through your body.

Damien squealed, completely like a pig, and collapsed to the floor. I thought I'd just crack him over the head and be done with it, but he started crawling down the stairs. I guess the whole "lower back disabled idea" wasn't entirely accurate. The more you know.

I wasn't expecting to have to chase after him so froze in my surprise, and before I knew it Damien had fumbled his way down the stairs and was standing up. I didn't have time to formulate a new solid plan so I just rushed him, grabbed him by the hair and pushed him through the sliding glass door. Well I tried to at least. I thrust him into the door and of course the door pushed back. There was a crazy loud crunching sound, like when you step on a beer can so it takes up less space in the recycling. I must've broken his nose or face or something, and he cried out a really pathetic, "OW-WWW". I would've laughed but I was too stressed about getting this done. It was a lot harder than just a couple good whacks with a bat. Also I'd dropped the bat when I rushed down the stairs, which was not the smartest move I've ever made.

My mind raced trying to figure out what to do. If I could get him out to the balcony I could at least just throw him over and maybe he'd land on his head in the street. But what if I couldn't get him through the glass? And if Damien tried to fight back, would I be able to take him? He didn't seem like the strongest fighter but I'm no heavyweight either. And my stupid move with the bat left me with only what I was born with. I gritted my teeth to keep the panic away.

Through all this I hadn't noticed that Stanley had risen from his post and come to watch the shenanigans. I caught a glimpse of his reflection in the glass staring at me, and his eyes seemed to say, "Yeah. Do it."

Maybe it was the adrenaline or maybe I just needed that extra bit of encouragement, but I grabbed Damien with both hands and found every ounce of strength in my body to get him through that glass door. He flew through it like it was water. The sound of it shattering and raining down on the hardwood floor was like a Christmas carol, and in my excitement I burst into a smile. This actually might work.

Of course I couldn't revel in my success too long. I followed him out onto the balcony where he was gripping the railing and panting, little spurts of blood covering his skin where the shattered glass tore at it. I pinched him under his armpits—which were weirdly sweaty, but maybe it's not so weird since I imagine getting attacked would make anyone anxious—and threw him into the air like a beanbag in Corn Hole. I was pretty impressed with the amount of strength I mustered up here. Before if you'd asked me to carry all the bags from a Costco shopping spree I would've looked around for a dolly to drag them on. Now I just threw a grown man (well grown in the age and weight sense, he was still wildly immature of course) clear into the sky. And Damien's no skinny young twink anymore, so it was quite a feat. No offense to him, that feels like a low blow in spite of everything.

The sight of Damien sailing through the darkness in his kimono and colored tighty-whities felt like a dream. I watched with a strange distance, as if I'd inhabited someone else's body who'd actually done this. He just nearly missed a bunch of electrical wires that ran through the middle of the street, which I'm pretty happy about because watching him get electrocuted would've been traumatic for me. I hate when I see squirrels lying in the middle of the road after that happens to them. And don't people explode a little or spew out some of their guts when that happens? No thank you.

He twisted and turned in the air, somehow getting his legs over his head, and he landed straight on his skull like I'd hoped with a pretty solid thud and an audible exhale of the air in his lungs. I watched his head bounce off the concrete, it looked like it hurt pretty bad. But I guess that's to be expected.

I stood over my execution and waited to feel something. I didn't have any regret, which I wasn't surprised about because I usually don't regret the things that I do. Of course I've never committed a murder before, but still I wasn't expecting to have a flood of unusual emotions. It was just done. Like when I finish cleaning the house, I don't have any great sense of accomplishment or appreciation. I complete what I need to do and move on. That's how I felt about this.

Stanley joined me out on the balcony and pranced along the railing. It seemed a bit precarious for him but cats are supposed to be agile, right?

He looked down at Damien then back at me. I feel like we had a moment of bonding through this, and I could finally see why Damien liked him so much. I went to pet Stanley but heard a large piece of glass crunch under my foot, and the sound echoed through the night. I staggered to get my foot off and instead of petting Stanley accidentally pushed him over the edge. He let out a little kitty screech all the way down. I tried to peer over to see if he'd landed easier than Damien but couldn't make him out in the darkness. I listened for a moment but realized I needed to make my getaway, so gave up on Stanley. Maybe tonight was a two-for-one special.

I made my exit by stepping carefully over the glass back into the house and retracing my steps through his bedroom. I went out through the patio again, which in retrospect I realize was unnecessary since in coming back down from the patio I walked right past the front door that was on the side of the house. But it seemed like a good idea at the time.

Stanley was sitting on the walkway right in front of the house and leered at me as I passed. Apparently our friendship was brief, which is understandable since from his point of view I just pushed him off the balcony.

I stopped a couple feet into the street to look at Damien. He was a few steps away and I could tell he was completely dead. His eyes were open but unblinking and his chest didn't rise or fall with any breath. He was completely still, and for once in his life he looked at peace.

In spite of all that he'd done and how awful I thought he was, I honestly hope this gave him some relief. I didn't do this to punish him, though he deserved plenty of punishment. I just needed him gone. Out of my life permanently, with no chance of coming back. And this was the only way to really ensure that. Well, maybe a little retribution too.

I walked back to my car and caught my reflection in the window. It seemed like it should be a moment where I really saw myself for who I am, finding some deep truth that would awaken me for the rest of my life. But what I saw was all the cat hair covering the stealth black turtleneck I bought to be covert. It was everywhere. I don't understand how it's even possible for me to accumulate that much cat hair seeing as how we had so little physical contact. Good that Stanley and my friendship's off, he's on my shit list now too.

I wonder if Damien has a lint roller I can steal.

THE AFTERLIFE

Wow you guys. Is it just me, or are they all more interested in talking shit than trying to figure out who murdered me? I know we've all got a lot of shit to talk but I'd make it a priority to find the guilty party if one of my friends was savagely attacked. Although I guess I can't claim all of them as my friends, and some I wouldn't want to (EILEEN), but still.

At least they didn't bring in some ridiculous detective with an exaggerated backstory meant to make him interesting. We all know detectives are meant to deliver the boring exposition, but giving one an absurd southern drawl like Daniel Craig and silly roundabout monologues about donuts and donut holes and donut holes within a donut hole is all much more obnoxious than engaging.

So yeah, the afterlife is real and I'm in it. But it's nothing like I ever pictured. I'd hoped that some baby-faced cherub would greet me strumming a tiny harp, whisking me away on a billowy cloud. We'd arrive at an overly ornate golden gate (not the bridge), one that would be the envy of everyone in Beverly Hills. They would swing it open for me as I sashayed through to find all the people I loved waiting for me (but the pretty Hollywood version of everyone—Marky Mark circa his Calvin Klein underwear ads would play me in this sequence, naturally), and we'd laugh and toast drinks in crystal Tiffany's flutes. But apparently the list of people who love me is dwindling if the actions of my supposed friends are any indication, so this party sequence needs a rewrite regardless.

Anyway, I was so very wrong about this, the afterlife. It's not even the blank white canvas where Harry had his weird retrospective with dead Dumbledore (spoiler alert). It's exactly what you're living, right now. I awoke (came to? resurrected? emerged?) standing over my inflated body. Not in the sense of my ethereal self stepping out of my corporeal body, I just...appeared there. It was very strange, it made as little sense as the rest of my living life. I wasn't covered in blood *Carrie*-style, thankfully, but I was in my painfully underwhelming outfit.

As I looked down on my carbohydrate-filled corpse, I had to stare beyond not the angelic abdomen of a twenty-something underwear model but the bloated belly of Danny DeVito. No disrespect to Danny DeVito—I live for *Matilda* and *Batman Returns*—but no one is bringing his picture to their plastic surgeon and asking to inject fat cells here, here and here so they too can have that body. And in all the sales pitches I've given myself about this moment, afterlife me was always way better looking than regular life me. Now I'm stuck with this gut and shitty old underwear for all eternity? Cool thanks.

On another note, I'd like to point out that my appreciation for Sarah Michelle Gellar is completely natural and in no way inappropriate. I'm a fan, sure, but I am by no means obsessed. And if everyone really took the time to get to know her oeuvre they would get why I like her so much. She's a fantastic actress, seems genuinely kind and gracious and honestly pretty funny, so what's not to love?

I'm actually really embarrassed that she got dragged into this. It's not at all how I wanted to have her in my life. Obviously I'm a real fan! That irrelevant comment was a stupid slip up, I don't even know why I said it. Obviously I didn't mean it. And I really hope they didn't show her pictures from the crime scene. I do not want her first and presumably only impression of me to be this broken bag of pasta laying in the street. Hopefully someone showed her that snapshot of me from Barcelona last summer. I was actually working out at the time so in as good of shape as I've ever been, and I was wearing the cutest sunglasses that I'd bought in this tiny store off a cobblestone street in Sitges, which I then stupidly forgot on the plane when I got back to LA. But I looked really good in that pic.

And not that I think she did do it, cause that would be really strange if she did, but what if she did it? What if Sarah Michelle Gellar killed me? How cool would that be! Obviously I would've rather gone out for a drink or brunch or something normal like that, but how many people can say they've been murdered by their celebrity gay crush? I wish she would've at least said hello or something first so I knew it was her.

So now I guess I have to figure out what to do here for the rest of time. Oh god that sounds like forever. You'd think they'd give out a handbook like in *Beetlejuice*. I wonder if my Apple TV works here, I could finish catching up on *Riverdale* finally. Can I even grab the remote? I have a lot of questions and apparently plenty of time to figure out answers. Is there really no one who can help guide me through this? An information center perhaps? If the train wreck that is LAX can figure out a welcoming situation for international travelers, surely the afterlife can come up with something. Maybe by the time I get to the bottom of all this, the police will have solved my murder.

Since my life had no closure I'd at least like my death to.

Oh also if anyone happens to be in the neighborhood sometime soon, will you make sure Stanley Kowalski's ok? He's stuck outside and he's not known for his survival skills. He's been described as Paris Hilton in feline form—useless and pretty bitchy. Despite what everyone says he's a very sensitive and delicate animal. I never realized how wildly misunderstood he is, everyone needs to stop being so reactive. Sure he can be a little stoic, maybe even stand-offish at times. But he also loves to cuddle and will follow me all around the house cause he never wants to be alone. He really is a wonderful pet and so not scary. Also, people—he's a cat. Let's not be dramatic.

Sorry one more thing, and I'm super annoyed about this. It took me forever to find a real copy of *My Fair Lady* on DVD, and of course two days after I find it on eBay this happens. I paid far more than I should've—I can't even admit how much it's embarrassing. But it's supposed to be delivered this week, so can someone return it and make sure they refund me? If I'm not going to be able to enjoy it I at least want my money back. Thanks.

Milton Keynes UK
Ingram Content Group UK Ltd.
UKHW010647020624
443357UK00011B/235/J